Toni had never felt
so cherished before...

"Nick!" she gasped as he moved his body over hers and pressed his mouth hard over one quivering breast. A thrill shot through her, and the gnawing ache in the pit of her stomach eased with the promise of fulfillment. Her entire body tingled with rapturous expectation as her husband trailed kisses up to her chin, then took masterful possession of her mouth.

"Toni, I——"

The rest of his words were lost in the purposeful cough Toni heard coming from above them.

"Nick, there's somebody..."

Dear Reader,

Your enthusiastic reception of SECOND CHANCE AT LOVE has inspired all of us who work on this special romance line and we thank you.

Now there are *six* brand new, exciting SECOND CHANCE AT LOVE romances for you each month. We've doubled the number of love stories in our line because so many readers like you asked us to. So, you see, your opinions, your ideas, what you think, really count! Feel free to drop me a note to let me know your reactions to our stories.

Again, thanks for so warmly welcoming SECOND CHANCE AT LOVE and, please, *do* let me hear from *you*!

With every good wish,

Carolyn Nichols

Carolyn Nichols
SECOND CHANCE AT LOVE
The Berkley/Jove Publishing Group
200 Madison Avenue
New York, New York 10016

Second Chance at Love

FROM THIS DAY FORWARD
JOLENE ADAMS

**SECOND CHANCE AT LOVE
BOOK**

To Ken Harper,
who shared in my dream,
and Helen McGrath,
who helped to make
the dream come true.

FROM THIS DAY FORWARD

CHAPTER ONE

"I CAN'T IMAGINE you wanting to stay single, Toni. You're too pretty...and you're rich besides." Smiling indulgently, Catherine Mercier reached across the table and patted the hand of the dark-haired young woman seated across from her. "Believe me, pet, marriage with the right man is a delightful institution. You just had a bad experience—that's all."

Toni shook her head in mock disgust. "Three things you never fail to remind me of are that I'm pretty by virtue of being your daughter, that I'm rich, and that all men aren't like Bob." Smiling, she glanced up as the waiter set her coffee in front of her, and thanked him.

"The trouble with you, mother, is that you're a born flirt, and you adore *all* men," she teased the moment the waiter was out of earshot. Her grey-green eyes deepened to emerald in amusement.

"I am not!" her mother protested. Then she smiled,

and winked at Toni. "And there are several men I don't like at all, darling. Besides my marvelous ex-husbands, that is." Her jawline tightened angrily. "And one of those I most despise is that . . . that . . . that—" She took a deep breath and exhaled in a hissed, "Nicholas Caldwell!"

Toni laughed softly. "Nick Caldwell would be simply crushed to hear that, I'm sure."

Catherine's blue eyes flashed. "Don't be flip, Antoinette!"

Antoinette. Nick Caldwell must have somehow managed to get under her mother's skin—no small feat that!

"All right, mother, tell me about Nick Caldwell," Toni said patiently.

"Later, Toni," Catherine said, half-turning to signal the waiter. She ordered bacon and eggs with lobster sauce, a croissant with butter, and a glass of grapefruit juice; then she turned to Toni and asked her what she would like for breakfast.

"Poached eggs, thank you," Toni answered distractedly. She frowned. Since she could remember, her mother had been on a perpetual diet. She had to be very upset to even think about eating all that food.

"Now, about that miserable excuse for a man," Catherine said, clasping her hands together and clenching them until her knuckles were white. "That Nicholas Caldwell!" She took a deep, deep breath, and exhaled very slowly. "He's a horrid man, Toni, probably the only one I can think of who's more arrogant than your former fiancé."

Toni smiled inwardly. If Catherine's description was even half accurate, then Nick Caldwell must be pretty intolerable.

Breakfast was served. They ate in silence with Toni

watching her mother closely, suddenly anxious to know what scrape she had gotten herself into this time. Was it money again? she wondered.

But of course. It was always money with Catherine, or rather the lack of it. There never seemed to be enough of it to satisfy her. Although a box-office "heavyweight" who could demand big money for all her films, Catherine was always in debt. She was outrageously impulsive, and notorious for sponsoring fly-by-night ventures that were almost always spectacular flops.

Toni still remembered with a shudder the time Catherine thought she had found *the* inventor with *the* invention that would put both him and her on Easy Street for the rest of their lives. She had blithely "borrowed" the stake the hapless fellow needed from Toni's accounts. Only by artful and deliberate contrivance by Toni's San Francisco lawyers had they been able to keep Catherine from being prosecuted for embezzlement. As a result of that little escapade, Catherine had been removed as trustee of her daughter's fortune.

"Ooh, I could kill that man!" Catherine's voice, ice-cold with fury, exploded into Toni's thoughts.

"Who?" Toni glanced around her, looking for the object of Catherine's wrath.

"Can you imagine him telling *me* that I could not ship my menagerie on *his* ships? I needed them for a new film. The nerve of him!"

Toni relaxed somewhat. At least it wasn't *money* this time. "No, mother, I can't." She truly could not imagine any man saying no to the stunning blonde woman who was her mother. Catherine would just not allow it!

Toni smiled as she continued, with only mild interest. "I didn't know Caldwell owned a shipping line, too."

She smiled tiredly. Steel plants, boiler factories, and now a shipping line. "Is there anything that man doesn't own?"

Catherine gave a sharp little laugh, then said simply, "Yes. *Me*."

"You? Oh, mother, really! *You* and Nick Caldwell?"

"Well, why not? He's at least thirty-five if he's a day!"

Toni chuckled. "And you are the mother of a twenty-five-year-old!"

Catherine quickly defended herself. "You don't look a day over eighteen."

"That doesn't keep me from *being* twenty-five," retorted Toni, enjoying the exchange.

Catherine forced a little laugh. "If we don't change the subject, and pronto, my love, you might not live long enough to reach twenty-six."

Toni grinned. "Tell me about Nick Caldwell then, mother. I mean, since you've met him face to face. Is he so good-looking as he seems to be in all those magazines and newspapers?"

"Please, Toni, you know I prefer you to call me Catherine," said her mother. "And yes, he's extremely good-looking, but he's very conceited about it."

Rich, handsome, women throwing themselves at his feet at every bend in the gold-paved road he traveled ...why shouldn't he be conceited? Toni thought with a grimace.

"But enough of him," said Catherine, pushing abruptly away from the table. "Let's take one last turn around the French Quarter before I have to catch the plane for L.A." Here her voice was heavy with gloom, though Toni knew her mother would never sacrifice the glamour of her life for the hot, sleepy days of New Orleans. "The only thing

California has going for it over New Orleans is the fact that Nick Caldwell isn't there."

Toni's interest was piqued. "You mean he's here?" Of course—her mother wouldn't have come all this way just to visit the old town, or her daughter, for that matter. No wonder Catherine was in a bad mood. She'd probably been angling to hook Nick as her new husband and been very recently rebuffed.

"Yes, dear," said Catherine. Then her celebrated blue eyes glinted colder than sapphires. "But that needn't concern you."

Toni sighed softly. The killer instinct that had made her mother a star spilled over a little too often into her personal life. Not that Catherine's jealousy really mattered. After all, she had about as much a chance of running into the infamous Nick Caldwell as into a blizzard here in New Orleans.

Toni stretched lazily, then flopped onto her stomach and continued to read. Except for going to the French Market one day, she had done nothing but eat, sleep, and read since her arrival in New Orleans. Fannie, who had been her baby nurse and surrogate grandmother since Toni was a toddler, was happy to have her home, but made no bones about the fact that she suspected Toni was still "moping" over Bob Carlson, whom Fannie had never liked. No number of denials could change her mind.

Fannie stood at the door, leaning her short round figure against the doorjamb, her brown arms folded and resting on her ample bosom.

"Lazy girl, you get up and you get out into the sun and fresh air. I'll not let you lie around my house, hiding your pretty face in a book."

Toni sat up and leaned her back against the tufted

white vinyl headboard. "I'm not hiding, Fannie. I was reading."

"Well, you'd better put that book down and go buy some clothes. Heaven only knows when your mama will think to ship your things! And just look at you. I've seen you in those same pants and shirt two days now. You get going, and buy something pretty." Her tone was imperious, and from past experience, Toni knew she would be well advised to do as Fannie suggested, or suffer hearing about it until she did.

"I suppose you're right," she conceded reluctantly. "But I'll have you know that these jeans are not the ones I was wearing yesterday; and yesterday's shirt was blue, and *this,*" smoothing down her knit top, "is turquoise."

"Well, they all look the same to me," said Fannie unyieldingly. "And it wouldn't hurt you to have a skirt and blouse, just in case you decide to join me in church. . . ."

"Okay, okay," Toni laughed. "You've convinced me!"

A half hour later, Toni was maneuvering Fannie's Fiat through the D. H. Holmes parking garage. She'd decided she would make the rounds of all the department stores on Canal Street on foot and then conclude her shopping trip back at Holmes with the purchase of one of her childhood favorites, coconut macaroons.

She made her way through the crowds on Canal and entered Maison Blanche. Since the first-floor cosmetic and jewelry counters were crowded, Toni passed them by and took the escalator up one flight to the sportswear department.

She emerged from the fashionable store an hour later, loaded with packages, her feet aching. Maybe Fannie has a point, she thought to herself ruefully. If she shopped more frequently, she'd probably be in better condition, in addition to having a more appealing wardrobe. She spied the K & B drugstore next door to Maison Blanche and slipped inside just long enough to refresh herself with a nectar soda—she knew if she sat at the counter any longer she wouldn't be able to get up. Crossing Canal Street, Toni headed for Godchaux's. Cool, quiet, and elegant, Godchaux's was exactly what she needed at that moment. She enjoyed browsing through the fine jewelry and scarves, and settled on a burgundy silk ascot to go with her new grey suit.

After a quick stop at Gus Mayer, Toni turned back toward D. H. Holmes and her beloved macaroons. She walked quickly through the large cosmetics department to reach the bakery located in the back of the first floor. As the cashier handed her the box of macaroons and her receipt, Toni smiled to herself—now that she'd bought something at Holmes, she could have her parking ticket stamped and wouldn't have to pay for parking in the store's lot. Heiress or no heiress, free parking wasn't all that easy to come by nowadays!

With the small box of macaroons perched precariously on her other packages, Toni exited through the back door of Holmes and headed toward Bourbon Street and the parking garage. The fact that she really couldn't see over the pile of boxes didn't bother her too much—until she collided squarely with a man coming from the opposite direction.

"Oh, no!" she gasped as her feet flew out from under her. Ironically, her only thought as both she and her packages hit the pavement was that the macaroons would probably crumble.

She sat amidst her scattered packages, for a moment too stunned to do more than stare at the shiny black shoes of the man who had knocked her down.

"Why don't you watch where you're going?" she demanded shortly, lifting her face to the cause of her discomfort. Then she blushed deeply. The man was none other than Nicholas Caldwell, looking down at her with undisguised amusement in his gold-flecked green eyes. His photos certainly didn't do him justice, she thought sourly, for despite her annoyance, she found the tall man standing before her devastatingly handsome.

"Why don't *you* watch where *you're* going?" he retorted, and now she was sure that he was laughing at her. Strong hands moved under her elbows, and she was lifted effortlessly, though gently, to her feet. "After all, you were the one walking against the flow of traffic," he added in a voice that was provocatively soft.

Putting a hand to her seat with an expressive wince, Toni glowered at him. Of course he would find humor in their collision. *He* had not landed on his bottom! Shrugging off his helping hands, she stepped away.

"Aren't you even going to thank me for helping you up?" His mouth quirked with a grin, and his eyes danced with amusement.

"Whatever for?" Toni wrinkled her nose, hating and liking his lopsided grin at the same time.

"At least apologize for your inattentiveness," he coached good-naturedly. "After all, you really weren't paying attention." He bent down to pick up her packages.

"Don't bother!" The sharpness in her tone embarrassed her, and she blushed again. "I can pick them up myself," she added in a quieter tone. "Just go away and leave me alone."

Dark, peaked eyebrows rose swiftly, questioningly. "Lord, I'm only trying to help you. What makes you so damned unfriendly, anyway?" Disregarding her protests, he bent and picked up her packages. "Is it that you took an instant dislike to me?" he asked doubtfully. "Or . . . is it that you hate *all* men?" he added wickedly.

Toni blushed. The fact was that he had her heart and pulses racing wildly, and she did not like the feeling. Worse, she suspected he knew exactly what he was doing to her . . . and was enjoying it!

"May I have my packages?" She held out her arms.

"Say please, and maybe I'll give 'em to you."

Glancing up quickly she caught a roguish gleam in his eyes and cringed. Her heart traveled rapidly up to her throat and proceeded to thud against her voice box.

"All right," she whispered hoarsely, *"please* may I have my packages?"

"That's better." He gave her back her boxes. Toni hugged them to her breast and, turning sharply on her heel, she tried not to run.

Whew! Her mother was right about him. He really was a most disturbing man!

"Are you always so damned rude?" Nick's deep voice cut into her thoughts as he came up beside her. Startled, Toni missed a step and stumbled against him. He steadied her, then set her gently away from him.

"Didn't anyone ever teach you to say thank you?"

Toni nodded behind her packages.

"Well?" The demand was made in a rather sharp tone.

Toni stopped, shifted her packages to look at him, and found that she had to tilt her head back quite far in order to meet his eyes. "Look, will you *please* just go away?"

"Ah, she does say *please,* and quite prettily, too," Nick teased, grinning down at her. "It's a free country, true? And this street does not belong exclusively to you, true? So—" smiling, he spread out his large hands and shrugged, the smile widening on his lips, "I can walk on it if I feel like it, true?"

Toni suppressed an urge to laugh by pursing her lips. "True. True. *And* true. But *I* do not have to walk with you." She hurried across the street.

"Do you know who I am?" he shouted, keeping pace with her on the opposite sidewalk. The remark drew a few snickers from passersby, but he seemed oblivious to them.

Cheeks flaming with embarrassment, Toni turned slowly to glare at him, ready to puncture his overinflated ego by claiming that she certainly had no idea who he was. But it struck her that, audacious as he was, he would probably cross over to introduce himself. At the moment, the last thing she wanted was to be seen with him. Nick Caldwell had an uncanny knack for attracting bad press.

"Of course I do," she shouted back. "Who doesn't?" She felt like a complete idiot when people gathered behind her to witness, and laugh at, their exchange. Then she knew what would get him. "And who cares?" she added at the top of her voice.

Her ploy worked, and Toni stared at him in amusement. He seemed to be brooding as he turned his back to her. There was, she had to admit to herself, a certain appeal in that indolent stance as he pretended interest in something in the store window. He appeared younger than the thirty-five years Catherine claimed he was, but then, she had never been a good judge of age.

"Ah, well," she sighed, and hurried away. She'd never

see him again, that much was sure. And she wasn't sorry, not in the least. Bob had given her enough heartache for a lifetime. And he had seemed so safe, so predictable. If she had misjudged Bob so badly, she'd be an utter fool to tangle with someone as dangerous as Nick Caldwell.

With a tinge of regret, Toni slipped into her car. Only this morning, she mused, she had been more or less indifferent to the shopping expedition. Now, inexplicably, Toni could not wait to show off her elegant figure in some of the stylish new clothes she had bought.

Toni was just signing the guest book at the end of her tour of the 1850 House on St. Ann Street when she sensed someone watching her. Glancing up from the brochure in her hands, she found Nick Caldwell barring her way. She stared at him, annoyed, yet strangely pleased.

"Who the hell are you, anyway?" he demanded. The amusement was gone from his eyes. In its place was only an intense curiosity.

For an instant Toni considered telling him that she was Catherine Mercier's daughter, but promptly changed her mind. Catherine would somehow hear about it and come down on her like a ton of bricks. That the glamourous Catherine Mercier had a daughter of twenty-five was a secret guarded more closely than the gold in Fort Knox.

"Nobody," she replied simply, and tried to squeeze past him.

Nick frowned. "Is that how you really feel about yourself?" One corner of his mouth lifted in a sardonic smile.

"Not at all," Toni rejoined. "I merely meant that I wish to remain nobody to you."

Again that sardonic lifting of his mouth. "And is there nothing I can do to make you change your mind?" His eyes roamed boldly over her slender form with an intensity that Toni found disquieting.

She set her jaw. "Look, Mr. Caldwell, I don't mean to be rude, but I don't want to be seen with you. I cannot afford the notoriety that follows an association with you, however inno——"

"Hold on, there!" he interrupted savagely, eyes glittering like those of a cat about to pounce on a defenseless mouse. "You're not holding me responsible for whatever trash you read in those stupid rags, are you?" He nodded his dark head toward the folded *Jet Setter* sticking out of her shoulder bag.

"Of course not," Toni taunted softly. "After all, they *never* print the truth, do they?"

His eyebrows jerked up in surprise. He regarded her soberly for a moment, and Toni studied him openly. His clothes, his air, gave him a look of intense virility, a sort of careless—and devastating—charm.

And *dangerous*, Toni added. She recalled the interview his then-current lover, Priscilla duPrie, had given for the issue of *Jet Setter* in her bag. The woman had admitted stealing and wrecking his car because he had dumped her in favor of someone named Nancy Kincaid. *Christine Banning. Priscilla duPrie. Nancy Kincaid.* And all in less than a year. It was no wonder Catherine called him a philanderer!

"After all," she continued, "you're certainly not responsible if some women can't cope with your rejection of them, are you?"

"What the—! Ah, I get it. You read Miss duPrie's fabrication of our, er...association."

"And, of course she was lying," Toni said with a catty sweetness rare to her. She gave him a brief smile and walked away.

He was immediately beside her. "Tell me, Miss Nobody, would you steal a man's car and run it into an embankment or do something equally destructive if the man chose *not* to become involved with you?"

"Good heavens, no. Can't you tell, Mr. Caldwell, I try to lead a quiet, private life. More than anything, I dislike extravagant gestures—and emotions." Toni blinked demurely, beginning to enjoy the exchange despite herself. "So you see, I'm hardly likely to find myself in the situation you describe," Toni concluded, an amused smile curving her lips.

To her surprise, Nick did not reply. But his green eyes narrowed with intensified interest, the color of turbulent seas. For a moment she met his gaze, and the superficial pleasure she had felt in bantering with this handsome man faded. She felt bewildered, stripped of all her usual defenses. She quickened her step to get away.

He matched her pace, and they reached the corner of St. Ann and Decatur streets in silence, a silence so tense Toni grew quite nervous. She wanted nothing more than to escape Nick's dark and brooding presence, so she hurried across the street, convinced she could lose him in the French Market. But she heard his firm footsteps moments before his deep voice whispered in her ear, "At present, I have in my personal account somewhere in the vicinity of ten million dollars, give or take a mil."

Now, *that* is a novel approach, Toni thought as she turned to him with a silent laughter expressed in her grey green eyes. "So little?" she teased.

"It means nothing to you?" His expression told her he did not believe her indifference.

Toni shrugged. He couldn't be serious. Was he testing her?

"Should it?" She moved away, pretending interest in the lettuce bin.

"Yes," he countered without hesitation. "Unless, of course, *you* have *eleven* in *your* account," he mocked, laughing.

Toni joined in his laughter, but for an entirely different reason from his. The image she had been coached to project since childhood was now second nature to her. No one suspected that she might be worth several million dollars. She dressed simply by choice, and since she shied away from reporters, very few people would recognize her on sight as the MacGregor Mills heiress. Those who did considered her eccentric—after all, why would someone obviously set for life subject herself to the rigors of law school?—and were glad to leave her alone.

"Eleven million," she said airily, giving her head a haughty toss. "That's about right—give or take a couple thou'."

"Between us, then, we could have a tidy little bundle," Nick quipped with a low, husky chuckle. "Now, how about my spending a couple of dollars on some coffee and sandwiches?"

"It's your money, Mr. Caldwell. Feel free to do with it as you please," Toni remarked sweetly as she started to move away from him. "And now, I'm late for an appointment. Good day to you, Mr. Caldwell."

"Wait!" Nick called out as Toni dashed across the street just before the light changed, and his pursuit was stopped by the oncoming traffic. "I don't even know who you are!"

"How unfortunate!" she called back to him, then followed the words with a peal of silvery laughter.

Her escape successful, Toni smiled ruefully. She realized that her light exchange with Nick back on the street corner contained more than a grain of the truth. She *was* afraid of raw emotion.

Even in high school, she'd felt more comfortable going out with guys who were bland and unthreatening. Just like Bob, she mused, as she began to stroll thoughtfully back to the house. She supposed all the tumult in her childhood home—though you could hardly call it a proper home—had helped to make her this way. With no less than four fathers by the time she was sixteen, it was hardly surprising that she didn't put much store in romance. Up until recently, she didn't think she was missing anything. Now she wasn't so sure.

Nick Caldwell was just too good-looking—and unpredictable—for comfort. The feel of his stormy eyes on her body did extraordinary things to her pulses. No man had ever affected her that way before, not even Bob.

CHAPTER TWO

Around seven o'clock one evening, Toni left the house, breathing a sigh of relief as the evening air caressed her cheek. For the past ten days, she had tried very hard to forget her two whirlwind encounters with Nick Caldwell and the disturbing emotions that had been left in their wake. At first flashes of memory took her by surprise. She would be doing something quite innocent and ordinary, like brushing her teeth, and she would suddenly sense Nick's presence, feel his bold eyes caress her. Gradually she succeeded in banishing Nick from her mind, but she was plagued by a moodiness that was new to her, feeling alternately restless and agitated. Tonight was no exception, and Toni felt especially at loose ends since Fannie had left town for a few days to visit friends.

Toni wandered aimlessly for a while in the general direction of the French Quarter, then found herself passing a charming outdoor café. Gratefully, she sat down at one of the little wrought iron tables, leaning back to enjoy the colorful street scene. An attractive young couple was approaching, quite obviously in love. In response to some teasing comment, the woman started to muss her lover's hair. His arms encircled her slender waist, and leaning back, he whirled her around. They were both laughing, in a golden world apart from Toni's.

As Toni watched the scene, a dull ache filled her. She forced herself to look away, picking up and studying the menu that had been handed to her.

She summoned the waiter. "Just coffee and a fruit salad, please."

"That's hardly good fare for an active woman," teased a deeply masculine voice from behind her. Toni swirled round to find Nick Caldwell standing there, smiling down at her. "It's taken me some time to find you again, but if you'd rather I leave. . . ." His expression told her he would rather stay.

"Well, should I leave?"

Toni opened her mouth, closed it. Why was her impulse to be so uncharacteristically rude to him? After all, what harm could come of having a cup of coffee with him?

"No, don't leave. Please join me." Smiling diffidently up at him, she held out her hand. "I'm Toni MacGregor."

"Actually, I already know," he replied with a dazzling smile, taking her hand.

"But . . . how did you find out?" Toni was puzzled.

"Well, I suppose I might as well confess," Nick said in mock penitence, still holding her hand. "But only if you promise not to send me away."

"What on earth are you talking about?" Toni shook her head in exasperation, gently disengaging her hand.

She never knew what Nick would do or say next.

"As you may have gathered, I'm not used to women running away from me. When you disappeared on me for the second time, I tried to convince myself that I didn't care. But a week went by, and I found myself hoping that I would run into you. And I still remembered the adorable way you have of wrinkling your nose when you're feeling suspicious. That's it—you're doing it again," Nick exclaimed, reaching across the table and gently stroking the bridge of Toni's nose. She began to smile broadly. She couldn't help it.

"So I went back to the 1850 house and found your name and address in the guest book. I was planning to look you up—honestly I was," he protested in response to the dubious look on Toni's face. "But I had the good fortune to find you here first," Nick concluded with a shy smile.

Toni's heart was racing madly. Did Nick really mean what he said? Before she could find her voice, he changed the topic abruptly.

"Now, Toni MacGregor, I'm going to order something more substantial for us to eat." A nod of his dark head brought the waiter immediately to their table.

"*Gigot d'agneau avec haricots verts à la crème, riz pilaf.*" After choosing a bottle of vintage Bordeaux, he turned to Toni and smiled. "I'm sure you'll like the roast leg of lamb here. It's a specialty of the house."

Hmm, thought Toni. So far he was just as Catherine had described him: persistent, charming, and, now, arrogant. To top it off, his French, like everything else about him, was perfect. It was almost demoralizing, and Toni felt she had to assert herself. "And if I don't like it?" she quizzed.

"I beg your pardon?"

"I'm sure you should! You tell me I'll like what you just ordered as though I have no other choice."

Nick blinked. "Lord, that wasn't my intention at all!" His eyes latched onto hers for a long silent moment, and she felt her cheeks begin to burn. He sheepishly agreed that he might have been just a teensy bit high-handed.

"Teensy bit!" she repeated hotly, and he grinned.

Toni found his grin infuriating, but that was soon to be the least of her worries. Nick fell into a watchful silence, and seemed to be studying her as though he were trying to make up his mind about something that involved her.

Or maybe he was just trying to remember if and when he had seen her before? Did he connect her with Catherine Mercier, she wondered. Toni distracted him by asking if there was something wrong with her face. "Is it my nose? Too short, I suppose," wrinkling her small nose, "or perhaps it's my mouth—too wide, eh?" Laughing nervously, she twisted her full lower lip to the side.

"Oh, no! Both are delightful! In fact, you're almost too beautiful to be real," he added as if talking to himself. "And you damn well know it, so quit fishing for compliments, Toni MacGregor," he teased after a moment, but his voice seemed humorless to her.

Toni colored. She hadn't been fishing for compliments—goodness knows she'd received more than her share in the past. It was just that she found Nick's silences maddening and felt she had to say something . . . anything. When they were chatting, Toni felt relatively calm and in control, but with Nick's eyes on her, she was bewildered by an unfamiliar rush of feeling. But before she could correct his impression of her, the waiter interrupted with their meal and Nick turned his attention to the food.

Toni tried a few delicious mouthfuls, then sipped the wine, watching Nick as intently as he had earlier watched her. She was too nervous to really eat.

"All right, Toni." Nick carefully set down his fork and propped his elbows on the table, clasping his hands together and resting his chin on them. "You have been staring at me long enough. It must be my face. Is there something wrong with it?"

Toni gave him a wide, innocent look. "No. Why? Is there something about your face you don't like?" she asked, as the beginnings of laughter deepened her dimples.

Nick started. "Brat! There's no way I can answer that without sounding vain, and you know it!" Good-natured lines crinkled at the corners of his eyes, and his smile was warm, considering he knew she had set out to annoy him. Toni sighed deeply. The man was just too self-assured.

"Now eat your dinner, Toni," he urged quietly. "Later, we can take a walk and then we'll talk. I have a . . . proposition to make to you."

Proposition! Toni's eyes turned dark grey with surprised dismay, and her mother's words rang hatefully in her mind: "Nick Caldwell is a philanderer, and if you ever meet him, I hope you have the good sense to steer clear!"

Strangely, she felt sick with disappointment, and she realized it was because she had nurtured a secret hope that Catherine was wrong about him. Then anger drove away the disappointment, and she dropped her fork to her plate. If he thought he could buy her for the price of a meal she had not even wanted, he could think again!

She stood up, stepping away from her chair as she

prepared to take flight from this obnoxious man. "I should have known," she muttered in a rueful tone. "I——"

"Sit down, Toni," he murmured softly, but firmly.

Toni sent a longing glance at the street beyond. She wanted to run, not because she was frightened of his physical strength, but because Nick Caldwell had an unnerving effect on her. But instead of running, she automatically obeyed him, for instinct warned her that he would not allow her to walk away from him a third time.

"What sort of proposition do you have in mind?" she demanded in a surly whisper, glaring at him.

"Ah-ha. Finish your dinner, then we'll amble on to the French Quarter." His lip curved in that lopsided grin that played havoc with her pulse. "I've been told it really heats up at night."

Toni's mouth curled contemptuously. Perhaps he was hoping she would be mesmerized by the candlelight, the neon lights, the blaring of jazz in the quarter and, of course, his own inimitable boyish charm, long enough to lend herself to a little fling with him. She thought about telling him that he had overestimated his attractiveness, but decided to keep silent.

"I hope the wine's to your liking, Toni," Nick said.

Toni managed a nonchalant shrug as she lifted the glass to her lips.

"Well?"

"It's all right," she passed judgment on the wine indifferently.

For a second Nick's eyes gleamed with cynical amusement, then his glass was lifted and he was making a toast to a long and pleasurable association.

"What sort of association?" Toni demanded warily,

feeling her stomach muscles become taut.

"A close one, I hope, Toni . . . and mutually satisfying." He smiled, and Toni's heart fluttered as the warmth of that smile extended to his eyes. Hand trembling slightly, she touched her glass to his.

"Mutually satisfying." The words rang in her ears as their glasses clinked, and she shivered at the sensual thoughts that raced through her mind.

Wordlessly, Nick paid the check and helped Toni from her seat. The New Orleans air was brisk this spring night, filled with the smells that wafted from within the restaurants. Toni shyly moved closer to Nick to stay warm as a chill overwhelmed her.

"Well?" Toni couldn't stand the suspense. "Are you going to tell me now what you want from me?" she asked.

For a moment Nick's eyes lighted up with mischief, then he sobered and said, "First you must promise me that whatever I say to you you won't take offense, for none is intended."

She eyed him suspiciously. "Ah-ha."

His eyes twinkled merrily. "All right . . . but first, show me your fingernails. Oh, those are nasty weapons," he teased, taking her hand. Toni's nails were long, carefully tapered, and painted an iridescent pink.

Toni quickly withdrew her hand, and lifted her brows in a gesture that was meant to be provocative, but to her chagrin he seemed to find it only amusing.

His smile was contagious as well as irritating. Toni felt her own lips twitching, and against her will she exploded into shaky laughter. "Oh, you're impossible, Nick Caldwell," she struggled against her laughter to say. "Look, it's cold out here. Won't you please—" She broke off when she felt something soft and warm falling lightly over her shoulders. Glancing down, she saw that it was Nick's coat. Grinning, he pulled it around her, holding it with one hand over her breasts. He drew her to him and looked into her eyes as he spoke.

"Now . . . you were saying?" What was that strange look in his eyes? Toni wondered if he was laughing at her again. She scowled up at him.

"No, *you* were going to tell *me* something."

For a moment he seemed to hesitate, almost as if he had changed his mind and was reluctant to admit it. Toni chewed nervously on the inside of her cheek, watching his face as she waited for him to speak.

"Marry me, Toni MacGregor."

The words were spoken so softly that at first she thought she had imagined them. Then she thought he was joking. Toni looked quickly into his eyes, but for once there was no sign of amusement in their green depths. She was stunned, and she knew her amazement could be read on every inch of her face.

"I'll be perfectly honest. I have to get married for business reasons. You see, more than anything, I want to be elected chairman of the board of Caldwell Industries, and I don't have a chance unless I'm respectably married. But that's not everything—by a long shot. Ever since I saw you, Toni, I just haven't been the same. So who knows what may happen once we get to know each other. Anyway, it will be fun, and no one but us need ever know that the marriage started out as an 'arrangement.'" Lifting his hand from his side, he reached out to smooth back a tendril of black hair that had fallen across her eye. "And I won't force you to do anything you're not ready for," he went on in a low, husky whis-

per. "And if you ever . . . want to go, you can slink quietly
out of my life. I promise you."

That did it! Toni took a deep breath to calm her racing
heart, and forced a smile that felt grotesque on her lips.
"You must believe I'm fresh out of kindergarten if you
think I'm going to fall for that line." Eyes darkening
with fury, she took a step back, slapping away the hand
that clutched his coat at her breast. The nerve of the man!
Slink away indeed! What did he think she was, a snake?

"You're crazy, Mr. Caldwell," she muttered as she
turned to go. And she herself must be a raving lunatic.
For a moment there she had found the idea of being his
wife frighteningly attractive!

"It's not a line, Toni," he called after her in a slightly
desperate tone. "In fact, I've never meant anything more
in my life!"

Toni ignored him and continued to put some distance
between them.

"You'll live luxuriously, Toni. You'll have anything
you want for as long as you remain my wife."

Toni froze. Slowly, she turned around to face him.
She stared at his sober expression and frowned. The man
was serious about this crazy marriage scheme!

He stood there, tense, waiting, the expression on his
handsome features that of a child who is hopelessly lost.
Suspicious though she was of his strange proposal, Toni
found herself aching to put her arms around him and
comfort him.

What was happening to her? She shook her head to
kill that frightening impulse, forcing her brain to function. She did not want a husband. She had sworn off
men, she reminded herself sternly. So . . . why, then, was
she still standing there?

Glancing up, she noticed she had unconsciously moved toward Nick; noticed, too, the intense look in his eyes, the strength in the hard line of his jaw.

Lord, she must be going crazy! To even think of playing such a game with this man was folly. She knew she was not strong enough to cope with his virile charm.

"Oh, God, why couldn't you have made your outrageous proposal to someone else? Why did you have to pick on me?" Before the words had fully escaped her trembling lips, Toni was running, and she did not stop until she was safely, breathlessly, leaning against the Fiat. Trembling hands fumbled with the key in the lock, got the door open somehow, and then she climbed in, her knees still shaking. For a minute, she just sat there, mentally replaying those insane last few moments outside the restaurant with Nick. She shivered. Reaching her hands up to rub some feeling into her goose-pimpled arms, she discovered she still had Nick's coat around her, and she marveled that it had stayed on her during her flight.

Impulsively, she nuzzled the butter-soft cloth with her cheek. The spicy cologne Nick used still clung to his coat, and suddenly she ached to touch him.

"Oh, God!" she moaned, for the moment shocked and disgusted at the intensity of her longing for the man. She had no intention of getting involved with anyone, let alone a playboy like Nick Caldwell. Hands none too steady, she reached down and turned the key in the ignition. But she did not start the car. Feeling emotionally washed-out, she leaned back against the headrest. Memories of the time she had spent with Nick flooded her mind and made her feel weak with longing. What had ever possessed him to propose to her? Closing her eyes, she could almost feel his hand clutching the coat at her breast, feel the warmth of his breath against her cheek. As she remembered the way she'd begun to sway toward him, her heart pounded almost painfully.

Shaking herself abruptly to clear her head, Toni reached down and started the car. But again she hesitated. Unable to understand her strange reluctance to go home, Toni turned off the ignition and leaned her elbows on the steering wheel, resting her face in her hands.

Against her will, her thoughts went to another handsome, dark-haired man, the man responsible for her wariness of men. Bob Carlson, her fiancé when she was in law school.

Toni raked her trembling hands through her silken, short black hair, trying to shake off the memories that crowded in on her.

She had been no misty-eyed teenager forming an infatuation for an older man when she'd met him; she was twenty-two, with college and one year of law school behind her. Catherine had introduced them. A lawyer, he worked for the firm she had hired to help her through one of her messy divorces. Though ten years older than she, Bob seemed to be the perfect mate for quiet, mature Toni. They discovered they enjoyed the same books, plays, films, sports.

Most important, however, they shared a love for law. Come to think of it, Toni had decided to become Bob's wife for the same reason she had decided to become a lawyer. Both seemed the natural choice, logical, predictable, and soothing. And for a while, solid, dependable Bob was a good influence on her. When studying became a chore, he was there, coaxing her out of the doldrums and encouraging her when she got stuck in her research. Bob always told everyone that theirs was a very modern relationship, with neither partner making demands on the other. It was he who decided they wait to marry until Toni was twenty-five, laughing as he declared, "There's no sense in having you lose your inheritance. Lord knows we'll need it to start our own practice. Just think: Carlson & Carlson; our own place in L.A., maybe, or even in good old San Francisco."

Toni swallowed hard and gave a small shake of her head, but nothing would chase away her memories. She rubbed her knuckles against her eyes and started the car again, her mind refusing to give up its wayward train of thought.

Just before she started her third and final year, Bob had suggested that they go visit Catherine's friends in Boston for one last relaxing vacation. He neglected to mention that he was planning to ask nationally known lawyer Gareth Talbot to take him on as junior partner in the prestigious firm started by Talbot's grandfather. And it wasn't until they were all gathered around the dinner table that he informed Toni he meant to use her inheritance to buy into the partnership.

"You won't mind that, darling, will you?"

Toni remembered how dry her throat had been on that occasion. Forcing the words through a scratchy throat, she gave him the answer he wanted. Later, she cautioned her furious mind, later she could ask him what had happened to his dream of opening his own practice. But later, he convinced her that if he became a part of Talbot, Talbot, Hill & Summers it would be the biggest coup of his career. To be known as one of that firm's partners would get him what he most wanted in life—recognition.

At first, Toni gave in gracefully. After all, she reasoned silently, what good was money if it couldn't buy someone she loved something he wanted so much?

But the more she thought about the whole idea, the more it rankled. Aside from the fact that she and Bob had planned to open their own firm, her career itself would now be delayed, and that could be deadly in a market being glutted by lawyers. For if the little deal were to go through, it would have to be at Talbot's convenience, not theirs—and Talbot wanted them re-settled in Boston within the month. It would take at least a year for a place in a Boston law school to open—if she were lucky—and the firm's image required that Toni be at her husband's side. In short, she couldn't remain the extra year in California to complete her degree. And the thought of waiting to finish up in a law school in Boston, and then encountering extra difficulty in using her hard-won skills, shook Toni's resolve to sacrifice her needs to those of the man she loved—a man who didn't seem to be giving her much love and consideration in return.

When she told Bob about her reservations, *her* needs, she was shocked at his reaction. He accused her of being manipulative, too demanding—after all, *he* was the man. She saw that she could no longer reason with him, that coming so close to satisfying what was obviously a life-long dream had made him deaf to any of her objections. Without further argument, she broke off the engagement.

Now, almost a year later, with her final year of law school just completed, she was running away from an-other man. Toni groaned, and stepped down hard on the accelerator. A vision of Nick Caldwell's smiling face swam unwanted before her tired eyes, and with another groan, Toni pulled the car to the side of the road.

In the last few months she had gone out with other men, had fielded a few propositions with good grace, and had even received a bona fide proposal of marriage. Common sense told her that not all men were like Bob, but emotionally she had been unable to cope with a close relationship, and when a man got that certain look in his eyes, she withdrew quietly and went into hiding.

She reached up to rub her arms. Nick's coat was still draped lightly across her shoulders. A fluttering breathlessness gripped her as thoughts of being held in his arms raced through her fevered mind. What was wrong with her! she demanded silently, angrily, of herself. Shaking her head, she told herself to forget Nick Caldwell, but she could not.

Suddenly she no longer wanted to deny that she was irresistibly drawn to Nick, the polar opposite of Bob: impulsive, spontaneous, and totally unpredictable.

After all, she could not just go home without giving him back his coat, could she?

"Who am I kidding?" she demanded derisively of the lovely oval face she saw in the rearview mirror. She was going back, and not just to return his coat.

"This is complete lunacy," she whispered as she turned the car around to go back. She felt a strange sense of calm wash over her. She was not insane. She knew exactly what she was doing.

She'd played it safe—or so she thought—in choosing Bob, and it had turned out that he was far more passionate about her money than about her. At least Nick couldn't possibly be interested in her inheritance—that much was clear. But what *did* he want? Toni wasn't exactly sure, but whatever it was she knew it would be dangerous, and exciting, and live. All her life she'd been such a good girl, and where had it gotten her? Now she was going to do something crazy!

She parked her car on Carondolet Street, and locked it. And then she was running back to where they'd parted.

"What took you so long, Toni MacGregor?" a familiar voice asked.

Relief washed over her. She hadn't lost him. He pushed away from the side of the building against which he had been leaning. Smiling, he held out his arms.

Toni made a skidding stop short of those inviting arms. "I c-c-came to return your coat," she stammered like an idiot, unable to admit that she had come back to accept his crazy proposal.

Nick laughed, a deep rich laugh that surrounded her with its warmth. "So where is it?" he demanded in amused mockery.

Toni reached up to her shoulders and found that his coat was no longer upon them. She smiled sheepishly, a soft coral flush of embarrassment shading her cheeks. "I guess somewhere between here and Carondolet Street."

"No matter," Nick said carelessly. He covered the distance that separated them in one long-legged stride. Trembling, Toni inched away from him. "No, Toni, don't you run away from me again. You came back to say 'yes' to me, and I'm not going to let you get away. I need you, Toni." Arms that were almost painfully gentle went around her, drawing her close. "I want you, Toni MacGregor."

CHAPTER THREE

THE LIVING ROOM in the house of the justice of the peace was modest, but Toni felt it was one of the most beautiful places she'd ever been. She sighed with quiet pleasure as she stood beside Nick. This was not quite the way she had dreamed her wedding would be, though she had no complaint to make about the groom. She stole a quick look at him, and her heart fluttered. Tall, proud, a faint smile curving his lips, Nick looked the picture of the contented bridegroom. A smile touched Toni's lips as she glanced down at the calf-length colorful skirt of Haitian silk and the matching peasant-style blouse Nick had bought for her to wear to her wedding. Her smile widened, and she only half listened to the man reading the marriage service.

When Toni had run back to accept Nick a few hours

before, she had experienced a drunken exhilaration unlike anything she'd ever known. Nick had insisted that they be married right away—he claimed he didn't want Toni to change her mind—and Toni was in no mood to oppose him. After all, once she'd agreed to go along with his crazy proposal, arguing over details would only spoil the enchantment of the moment. So they'd shopped for clothes in the French Quarter, then taken off in Nick's private jet for Las Vegas, where weddings at all hours of the night were commonplace.

Nick nudged her out of her thoughts, and Toni lifted eyes wide with surprise as the justice of the peace was prompting Nick to kiss her.

Good God! The ceremony was over and she hadn't heard any of it!

Nick's arms went around her shoulders. Smiling, he bent his head toward her.

"Oh, Toni, you've made me one happy man!" he said against her lips. He hugged her fiercely to him, kissing her with an intensity that left her quivering with feeling from head to toe.

He released her almost reluctantly. Toni looked around her in a daze, for the first time seeing the two witnesses standing immediately behind and to the left of the justice of the peace. Suddenly a horrible thought entered her mind. Had Nick's words and the lingering kiss that had left her lips tingling been only for the benefit of their audience? She felt a sadness that both confused and irritated her. Her eyes misted, and she was glad that Nick's back was now to her so he could not see the tears.

"Come, darling, our plane's waiting," he said, reaching behind him for her hand. "We're off to the Balearic Islands for our honeymoon, which, unfortunately, has

to be combined with business," he added as he slipped
a folded bill into the justice's hand.

Toni blinked. *Honeymoon*. Was it possible he was
considering the real thing? Sensations that were not totally unpleasant fluttered through her body, leaving her
trembling with a mixture of anticipation and apprehension. Color flushed her cheeks when Nick turned to look
at her.

"Ready?" he asked softly, holding out his hand to her.

Outside, the night air was brisk, but with Nick's arm
around her, Toni hardly felt the chill. And then, after
they'd caught a cab for the airport, Nick outlined the
plans he had made for their vacation.

Vacation, not honeymoon! Toni could feel only relief.

"We'll be staying in a friend's villa on the island of
Majorca," he said, using the Spanish pronunciation with
as much ease as he used French and English, Toni noted.
"They're off somewhere in Australia because Midge—
that's their daughter—needed to do some research for
a book." He chuckled. "Sure am happy she's not writing
about me. She's merciless when she goes after a story.

"Anyway, Toni, there are a lot of things I want you
to see." He glanced down at her, and for a moment
seemed content to just look at her. Smiling, he continued.
"I hope you like to poke through cathedrals and the like."

Toni nodded. With the daze her mind was in she
would have agreed to go trekking over the Sahara Desert
had he suggested such a thing.

Then the sight of a Fiat next to the cab made her
remember that she was part of the real world and had
real obligations. "Oh! Oh, Nick, I can't leave yet! I have
to tell Fannie, and then there's her car——" She stopped
abruptly at the look on his face.

"You know you can send Fannie a telegram, letting her know that you're safe, and explain later. Tell her where the car is, and don't worry—now that you're going to be my wife, you're never going to have to borrow anything, ever."

Oh, no, Toni realized with a shock, he'd thought she was only joking about the money in her account. He thought she was poor!

She hastened to explain. "Nick, I usually don't borrow things. I only did it this time be——"

Again he cut her off. "You'll like the kind of car I'm going to get you," he interrupted firmly, but his voice softened as he added, "and you can consider it a wedding present."

Then a melting look filled his green eyes. "Come here, you!" The command was a soft whisper, but the hands that reached out for her were hardly gentle. Delight and apprehension were intermingled in the shiver that trailed like cold fingers tripping up her spine. Then, his voice velvet soft, he said, "This Fannie . . . what is she to you?"

"Surrogate grandmother, companion, confidante . . . everything else you can think of."

"Are you an orphan, Toni?" His tone was unbelievably tender.

Ooops! Now was the time to open up and tell him that Catherine Mercier was her mother. What would he do? Stop the cab and demand she get out?

There was only one way to find out!

Although she experienced a faint queasiness in the pit of her stomach, Toni turned in her seat to face Nick, prepared, if slightly frightened, to share her secret. She opened her mouth and choked on her confession as Nick's arms closed around her and his mouth came down over hers.

An eternity passed while his mouth explored hers—an eternity loaded with explosive emotions that Toni could not understand. Frightened more by her own feelings than by what Nick might be able to do in the back seat of a moving cab, Toni squeezed her arms between them and pushed gently against his chest.

"Nick, there's something I have to tell you," she said nervously, trying to find the words to tell Nick about Catherine. But before she could think of a way to start, Nick interrupted.

"Never mind, Toni, I understand. You're not a child, and neither am I." His jaw tightened and for a moment she saw anger flare up in his eyes. Toni stared at him in confusion. What was he thinking? She opened her mouth to ask, and shut it. Whatever it was he thought he understood had made him angry, and if she were to ask him to explain, heaven only knew how much angrier he might get.

"Look, Toni," he said a few moments later, his voice infuriatingly calm, expression bland in his green eyes, "there is nothing you need to tell me. We both have a past, but let's not let it spoil anything. We will just start from today," he added, drawing her closer and brushing a kiss across her half-parted lips. Holding her away from him, he grinned into her confused expression. "There are, after all, a few things that should remain secret between a husband and a wife...especially in a case like ours."

With a sigh of relief, Toni pushed Catherine to the back of her mind, left the cab behind Nick, and followed him to his plane. Then, having settled herself comfortably into one of the honey-colored plush high-backed seats, she reached for Nick's hand. Soon after takeoff, with the soothing hum of the engines in her ears, she fell into a fitful sleep. But before losing consciousness, a disturbing thought presented itself to her exhausted mind: What if Nick wanted her to keep certain secrets to justify his doing the same?

"You know, I think I'm hungry," Toni told Nick as she came out of a wonderful dream that left her eyes liquid-soft.

Nick chuckled and lightly caressed her sleep-flushed face with the back of his hand. "It's no wonder, babe. You didn't eat anything at dinner." He smiled. "You were too busy devouring me with your eyes." Without giving her a chance to wake up fully and deliver some sort of sharp denial, he summoned the steward and ordered breakfast.

By the time the meal arrived, Toni was wide awake. The sun was just rising over an endless body of deep blue water, which Nick informed her was the Atlantic, and Toni felt a surging joy in her breast. Nick dismissed the steward, who disappeared into the forward cabin, and began to uncork a bottle of champagne.

"But Nick," Toni protested, shaking her head at the long-stemmed glass that Nick was offering her, "I only just got up."

"You just got married last night, remember? You can't have a wedding without a proper wedding breakfast, you know. I won't have it," Nick teased, lifting the glass to Toni's lips with a mischievous smile.

Toni had to admit the wine was delicious. Ravenous now, she turned to the silver tray in front of her: caviar with all the fixings, a plate of fluffy scrambled eggs, and tiny sandwiches of delicious smoked salmon on thin brown bread. She ate hungrily, and in silence, pausing now and then to steal a glance at her new husband. The meal was perfection, like everything that Nick did. Toni gave a sigh of contentment and reflected that it seemed as if she was going to enjoy her new life with Nick after all.

Sleepy again from the wine and good food, Toni dozed for a while after breakfast, her head nuzzled shyly against Nick's broad shoulder.

She awoke to find Nick gazing strangely at her. For a moment she thought he was in pain. Then he flashed her a glance that gave no hint of his thoughts and feelings.

"I'll be honest with you, Toni," he said quietly. "I came to New Orleans to make my pitch to a woman I've known for years . . . probably the only real friend I have in the world. Then, when I met——"

"You don't have to explain anything to me," Toni interrupted, her voice cold and sharp. Then, wanting desperately to hide her disappointment, she continued in a monotone, "I understand, Nick."

"Do you, Toni? Do you really see?" Keeping his eyes averted, Nick reached out blindly for her hand, and Toni let him hold it for a moment. "I certainly hope you do, Toni," he added, giving her hand a little squeeze.

Now she did see. Of course! She was his second choice. Toni was furious that it should bother her so. Good Lord, what else had she expected? That the notorious playboy Nick Caldwell had remained a bachelor all this time simply because he was waiting for her to come along?

Yes! cried her foolish heart. Oh, yes! And right now

CHAPTER FOUR

FIVE LOVELY DAYS of just lazing under the warm Mediterranean sun, of doing nothing but half-heartedly fending off Nick's playful attempts to seduce her, of Nick's pandering to her every whim, and Toni was feeling more than a little confused about her feelings. Was she beginning to fall in love with Nick?

No. It can't be. Not this quickly. Still...if Nick had meant for her to fall in love with him, he could not have picked a better spot than the island of Majorca to make it happen.

She'd been enchanted by his friend's villa the moment she saw it from the road. It stood on a rise overlooking the sea. Though less than forty years old, it possessed an old-world charm with its grillework, arches, and red-tiled roof. Inside, the house was furnished as scrumptiously as any small chateau might be, with thick carpets,

41

marble floors, crystal chandeliers and, everywhere, elegant statuary and antiques that the Mortons had brought
from France and England.

And this little cove where they had spent most of their
waking moments when they were not sight-seeing or
shopping for her new wardrobe—Toni was certain she
could stay here with Nick forever.

Lazily she rolled onto her back to soak up a little more
sun before going in for breakfast, and came full tilt
against glittering green eyes that had been studying her
with ferocious intensity. She smiled up at him while her
heart perversely began to pound against her ribs.

"You know, Nick, I was thinking—" She stopped as
Nick lowered his face toward hers.

"About what?" he drawled.

Toni took a deep, calming breath. "About being so
lazy," she lied, turning her face so that his kiss, aimed
unerringly for her mouth, merely grazed the line of her
jaw.

Nick laughed, and dropped down full-length on his
side beside her. "We could always do a little bit of pleasurable exercise," he suggested, running a teasing finger
across the exposed swells of her breasts, his eyes
wickedly intent on where his finger moved.

"Like swimming?" Her tone was falsely innocent.

"I had something else in mind," he retorted, bending
swiftly to steal a kiss from her parted lips.

"For instance?" she teased, moving out from under
his mouth.

"For instance, this. . . ." His mouth settled warmly
over hers; his arms went under and around her, drawing
her bikini-clad body against his own, nude except for a
pair of snug, low-riding brown trunks.

She was breathless, and he was grinning when he lifted his head from hers. "Well, what do you think of my suggestion, Toni?"

Toni opened her eyes wide. "What suggestion?"

Nick grinned. "Ah, the woman likes my methods of communication," he murmured as his lips came down to hers again.

Sky rockets flamed and exploded in her body as his mouth moved deftly over hers, and she knew that this time she would not refuse him. Sighing deeply in her throat, Toni arched her body to gain a closer intimacy. Nick moaned as her thigh came into contact with his manly hardness, and tightened his hold on her until she felt she could not breathe.

It was so natural that he should remove her flimsy bikini bra, so right that he should then lower his mouth to tease and caress the creamy-soft mounds arching provocatively toward his face. Not another person to be seen, not a murmur other than the gentle lapping of the sea onto the shore and the pounding of their two hearts. Toni had never felt so cherished before.

"Nick!" she gasped as he moved his body over hers and pressed his mouth hard over one quivering breast. A thrill shot through her, and the gnawing ache in the pit of her stomach eased with the promise of fulfillment. Nerve ends quivered; her entire body tingled with rapturous expectation as her husband trailed kisses up to her chin, then took masterful possession of her mouth.

"Toni, I——"

The rest of his words were lost in the purposeful cough Toni heard coming from above them.

"Nick, there's somebody . . ." she whispered huskily, dropping her arms from around his neck.

Nick lifted his face, green eyes snapping. "Yes, what is it?" he rasped out coldly. Toni shivered as she felt his body tense with anger.

The maid looked away in embarrassment. "There is a—" big pause while she searched for the proper word in English, "—an aunt of Señora Caldwell's in the *sala.*"

Aunt? Toni frowned. She had no aunts!

"Nick, I can't find my clothes," she hissed, turning her head to search the sand around her. Friend or foe, whoever had dropped in on them was not going to find her nude! "Get off the towel so I can wrap it around me!" She managed to squeeze her hand between them, and pushed against his chest, but he did not move.

"Did you invite your aunt here, Toni?" he mumbled, his tone heavy with reproach. The look he gave her showed her how unhappy he was at that moment.

Toni opened her mouth to deny even having an aunt when she heard her mother's voice floating toward them. She saw Nick's features tighten angrily and realized that he, too, had recognized Catherine's voice.

"So! It's true! God in heaven, how I wanted to believe that the papers were lying!" Catherine's voice whipped about them in practiced sorrowful tones. She came into view as Toni was struggling to push Nick off her.

"Antoinette! Oh, what have you done?" Catherine seemed to be highly scandalized at the scene that greeted her eyes. Covering her face with her beringed hands, she began to rock back and forth on her heels, moaning as though she were in excruciating pain.

When the initial shock of seeing her mother had passed, Toni found her performance amusing. An accomplished student of melodrama, Catherine had no equal when it came to histrionics. Struggling against a heady impulse to laugh, Toni turned to Nick and stiffened. His features were granite hard, and icy anger flared in the emerald depths of those green eyes that only a moment before had gazed so adoringly down at her.

Wondering if his anger was directed at her, Toni lifted herself to her knees, placing her free hand on his arm while her other hand held tightly to the towel she had wrapped around her.

"Is something wrong, Nick?" she asked inanely.

"Why the hell didn't you tell me?" he snarled, throwing off her hand.

Catherine stood very stiff in a black silk pantsuit that set off her pale skin and blonde hair to perfection, eyes glazed and staring off into the sea.

Toni turned back to Nick with a smile that was belied by the unhappiness that dulled her eyes. "You told me a wife and husband should have a few secrets from each other," she reminded him quietly. "Well, Catherine was my secret." Her smile faded under Nick's murderous glare.

"Nick, I'm——"

"You deceitful little bitch!" he ground out savagely. He sucked in air noisily and visibly tightened his jaw. "I'll be damned if I let this blasted marriage mean anything!" he finished in a whisper that washed over Toni like a pailful of iced water.

If his words stung, the fury she read in his eyes left her raw and bleeding. His accusation echoed eerily in her mind, and Toni winced involuntarily. She hadn't even known he was looking for a real wife! she screamed in her mind, but she could not force the words through a throat tight with hurt. Not that it would make any difference. She knew that nothing she said would sway

Nick now. With his arrogant chin held stiffly, Nick looked as stoic and unyielding as a Roman sculpture, she thought dismally.

Toni forced her attention back to her mother. An elderly man stood just behind Catherine. Heavens, it looked like the pictures of Guido deAngeli! It must be— short, balding, with thick lips and a bulbous nose. Toni knew only that he was an enormously wealthy Italian industrialist and that, if that ring shimmering on Catherine's finger represented a marriage, Catherine was his fourth wife.

"This is the child you spoke of, *cara?"* Guido asked in an incredulous tone, his small brown eyes boldly roving over Toni's near-naked form. "But she is a woman! You assured me your niece was a *bambina!"* Toni's cheeks flamed to match the color of her towel as his eyes zeroed in on the exposed swell of her breasts.

Toni's eyes went quickly to her mother, a beseeching expression darkerning them. Tell them, mama! she thought. For once in her life, couldn't Catherine admit that she was her daughter!

"But she's just a baby, Guido," Catherine snapped in self-defense, and Toni sagged with defeat. Sighing with exasperation, Catherine returned her gaze to the sea.

"You still can't say it, can you?" Toni muttered, and turned toward Nick, determined to tell him the truth when Catherine interrupted.

"Why else do you think I was distraught to find that she had married this . . . this—" She jerked her shoulders in anger, obviously unable to find a name vile enough to use on Nick, and pursed her lips in frustration.

Toni's eyes swung swiftly to Guido as he jeered, "Why, indeed?" His eyes contemplated the woman he

had married, and narrowed shrewdly as they slid to
Nick's implacable expression. "I hardly think we need
invent a mystery where none is needed," he commented
wryly.

Guido's smile was deprecating as he approached Nick
with outstretched hand. "My apologies, Caldwell, for
this intrusion into what must still be your honeymoon."
Distractedly he shook hands with Nick while his small
eyes resumed their insulting study of Toni's figure. "My
wife convinced me we came on a mission of mercy, to
save an innocent from the clutches of a sex maniac. But
Signora Caldwell does not appear to me to want to be
rescued, eh?" He muttered something in Italian, sliding
a venomous glance at Catherine.

"I have been made to look the fool," he hissed.

"You find yourself in good company, deAngeli," Nick
murmured, his mouth a taut line of anger.

"And I'm the biggest fool of the lot," Toni muttered.
"I was actually ready to buy this crazy marriage bit."
Grasping the towel firmly over her breasts, she spun
around on her heel and strode up the path to the house.
Her eyes were gleaming with tears, but she would not
give Nick the satisfaction of seeing how much he had
hurt her!

A gnawing in her stomach reminded Toni that she had
missed both breakfast and lunch. She left the room where
she had hidden for the better part of the day and went
in search of a maid to ask for a sandwich and a cup of
coffee.

"*Señora?*" A timid voice came to her from out of the
shadows, startling Toni.

"Oh, Maria, you startled me."

"Forgive me, *señora*..."

"You had something to tell me?" Toni prompted, experiencing a sense of doom.

"The *señor* said he was going out and did not know when he would be returning. He said for us not to wait dinner on him and"—she bowed her head in embarrassment, and continued in a faltering voice—"he said that you are not to wait up for him...." Her voice drifted away to an uncomfortable silence.

"Thank you, Maria," she dismissed the maid dully. Suddenly she had lost all desire for food. She felt an unsettling emotion in the pit of her stomach, but it was not hunger. Crossing her arms over her midriff, Toni pressed down hard to ease that awful gnawing sensation.

It took her a few moments to realize that she had been deserted. Could Nick have gone to another woman already?

Why should she care what he did, where he went, or with whom? Hadn't she known that Nick was a womanizer? Hadn't she convinced herself that since theirs was not a real marriage, nothing he did would ever hurt her?

Like it or not, irrational though the feeling was, the thought of Nick being with another woman made her furious. Anger soon gave way to hurt, and she negotiated the stairs up to her bedroom with heavy feet. They had made a bargain, and she would keep her part, but there was no sense moping around the house just because Nick was gone. Theirs was an arrangement, not a marriage, and she'd better get used to the idea and pick up the pieces of her life.

Taking a deep breath to steady her nerves, Toni wiped angry tears with the back of one hand and went into her bathroom for a bath.

Briskly toweling herself off, she returned to her bedroom. Crossing to her closet, she pulled out a full-skirted paisley print silk jersey gown that Nick had urged her to buy in Palma, and slipped it on before she could change her mind. Nerveless fingers shaded her lids with compatible teal and turquoise shadowing creams, then lightly tinted her trembling lips with coffee-color lip gloss. A quick comb through her feathered black hair, and she was satisfied with her appearance. She sat on the edge of her bed to put on nylons and shoes.

Sucking in lungsful of perfumed air, she walked out of the room, informed the first maid she saw that she was going out, and left the house. What was the point in feeling sorry for herself? She would go to the party that one of her mother's cronies, Margarita Fuentes, was having . . . the one Nick had refused to attend.

A dawn flushed with pink, mauve, and rose found Toni trying to steal back into the locked house without waking anyone. Courage magnified completely out of proportion by the excessive amount of wine that Margarita had encouraged her to drink, Toni skirted around to the back of the house and looked up at the windows, a crooked smile curving her lips when she spied the open window.

She chuckled. There was that obliging tree that grew near her veranda, its limbs shooting up to the sky before gracefully drooping down to kiss the ground.

Quickly removing her shoes and nylons, she threw down the hose and stuck her shoes in the belt of her gown. Hiking up her skirts, she gathered them, too, into her belt. Thank goodness she'd been a tomboy, she thought as she started up the tree. "A piece o' cake," she murmured moments later. She was sitting on a limb that seemed to reach all the way into her veranda.

Keeping her eyes on the wrought-iron railing she hoped to reach eventually, she lifted herself from a sitting position and crawled across the limb. Reaching the end of it, she found that there was a gap of about five feet to bridge. Shakily lifting herself to her feet, and fervently wishing for wings, she jumped. Even before she left the limb's flimsy support, Toni knew she had miscalculated.

Oh, Lord, don't let me fall, she prayed silently, holding her breath and furiously flapping her arms in an effort to grab the railing. Her fingers touched the cold iron, then she was grasping the top bar of the railing, clinging frantically to it while her legs swung uselessly beneath her. For one breathtaking moment she closed her eyes as the world swam dizzily below her.

An eternity flitted past as Toni clung desperately to that bar, too stubborn and proud to call out. Finally, she managed to hook one leg over the railing. For a moment she remained motionless, taking short gulps of air through her mouth to feed her oxygen-hungry lungs, then she scrambled for safety.

Safe now, Toni smiled crookedly, wondering what Nick and Catherine would think to see the enviable Mrs. Nicholas Caldwell III sneaking into the house at dawn via a second-story window. Settling down gratefully on the window seat, Toni paused for breath, her mind drifting back to the Fuentes party.

Nick knew the real reason behind Margarita's sudden and overzealous invitation, and that's why he'd turned it down, Toni remembered thinking the moment she entered the immense ballroom of the Fuentes villa. There had been a noticeable hush in conversation and a million eyes, or so it had seemed, had shifted to her as she walked across the room to greet her hostess. Margarita, a platinum blonde of indeterminate age, had waved away several young men crowding around her and immediately focused all her attention on Toni.

It had not taken Toni long to realize that her only attraction for Márgarita and her crowd—Catherine and Guido included—lay in the fact that she was Nick Caldwell's wife. Even then, she had no real draw as an individual, except that, under the guise of being Nick's friends and interested in his life, they had hoped to pump her for all of Nick's secrets. But Toni, accustomed to dealing with Catherine's crowd—and no fool—fielded their questions cautiously, feigning ignorance and naiveté until she learned all *they* knew about her husband, including the fact that Nick had married her in order to qualify for the position of chairman of the board of Caldwell Industries. So everyone already knew their marriage was merely an arrangement.

Throwing off her clothes, Toni moved through the dark room. Briefly closing her eyes to hasten their adjustment to the dark, she went across to the closet for her nightgown. She opened it and immediately realized that she was in the wrong room. Unsteadily, she turned to retrieve her clothes from the floor, and let out a small shriek as a dark blob separated itself from the corner of the room and started toward her.

It was Nick. The panic left her as swiftly as it had come. Toni stared in bemused silence as he came slowly closer.

"Hi, there." Toni grinned, looking up into his grim features, her senses too befuddled to realize that her husband was as angry as she would ever see him. She stretched lazily, the lacy fabric of her slip straining against her firm young breasts. "Mmmm, I'm all tuck-

ered out. I guess I danced with too many of Margarita's
fancy *caballeros,*" she yawned.

His jaw tightened, his fists clenched and unclenched
at his sides. "Had fun, did you?" His voice was dan-
gerously soft.

Finally, Nick's anger penetrated through the alcoholic
haze. Why, he was jealous, she realized, suddenly sober.
For a moment, she stood perfectly still, believing he
meant to strike her as he raised his hand, palm facing
her. She steeled herself to receive the blow. After all,
she reasoned illogically, the physical pain he would in-
flict would be nothing compared to the pain that had
been gnawing unmercifully at her insides ever since one
of Margarita's guests just happened to mention that she'd
seen Nick earlier that evening having dinner at a restaurant with a woman she gleefully identified as Nancy
Kincaid.

Her silence seemed to inflame him. Taunting her with
a contemptuous laugh, Nick swung her easily into his
arms, warding off her efforts to prevent him as he carried
her across the room. He dumped her unceremoniously
on the big bed, still neatly made.

As she made a mad scramble for freedom, Nick
reached down and grabbed a handful of silk slip. Toni
shrieked. Nick laughed harshly, yanking the flimsy fabric
away from her body. Toni's hands flailed in an effort to
cover herself, and again Nick laughed. His hard fingers
closed over her wrists, forcing her hands high above her
head. The full weight of his muscular body pinned her
to the mattress.

As she looked up at him, Toni realized that he had
become a stranger, a dark and brooding man she did not
know and could not like. His gaze—hard, ruthless—

bore down on her frightened face. Toni knew she was powerless against him, but still she was determined to thwart his intentions. She turned her head swiftly to avoid his seeking mouth, but he was ready for that little trick. Swiftly, almost effortlessly, he maneuvered her hands until both wrists were imprisoned in one large hand. His other hand cupped her chin and held her face beneath his. He looked long and hard into her eyes, a crooked smile curving his lips.

"Perhaps if I told you what I want from you, *in Spanish,* you would be more responsive to me, even eager for what I have in mind," he taunted cruelly as he took her mouth. Warm, moist, and tasting of whiskey, his mouth moved deftly over her pursed lips until he forced them open. His tongue went slowly in, exploring, teasing, robbing her of breath.

"Please, Nick, let me go," she begged, breathlessly, the instant her mouth was free.

"I thought you might prefer my kisses this way," he jeered cruelly.

Toni flushed hotly. It was true even then. She wanted his kisses, the caresses of those long sensuous hands, but not his anger. The blood pounded in her head as his hands began their sensual play over her skin, tantalizing, searing it with a fiery touch, arousing to a fever pitch of desire her shivering body. Ripples of ecstasy shot through her limbs, warming her, weakening her until every fiber in her body was quivering with the intensity of her feelings.

Toni knew if she did not move now, she would never want to leave his bed. Drawing in her breath against the weight of his face on hers, she renewed her efforts to break free. "Nick, this wasn't part of our deal!" she rasped out in desperation, pushing hard against his chest.

He ignored her plea. A knot of hurt formed in her throat, and the tears she had valiantly held back slipped unheeded out of the corners of her eyes. A sob rippled through her pursed lips, and her body shook uncontrollably beneath him.

"All right, Nick," she whispered, tone heavy with defeat, "do what you want, but do it knowing that I'll hate you for as long as I live."

"Oh, God!" he groaned as he flung himself away from her. He rolled on his side, and in one fluid movement he was off the bed.

A long shuddering sigh moved through her as his angry footsteps moved quickly away from the bed. She heard the bedroom door open, then close with a snap. Toni curved herself around the pillows and sobbed out her hurt.

CHAPTER FIVE

TONI ROLLED OVER onto her back and closed her eyes tightly against the ache throbbing in her forehead. The Mediterranean sun beat down, sending wide ribbons of dark gold brightness into the room, heating the breeze that awakened her. Almost immediately she remembered what had happened and felt hot with shame and confusion. The searing memory of Nick's brutal passion made her ache with desire; at the same time she hated him for what he had almost done to her.

Let him sink or swim on his own in the struggle for control of his grandfather's corporation, nagged a voice that suddenly erupted inside Toni's aching head. That part of her was all for packing her things and walking out on their agreement. The newspapers would have a heyday with the story, and any chance he might have had of winning the votes of the few straitlaced stockholders who wanted a "solid, feet-on-the-ground man to head the corporation" would go *pfft!*

"It would serve him right!" she sniffed.

But she would not walk out on him. She could not. She knew now that she loved him.

"Oh, no!" she moaned into the pillow, pained by the truth that had come from somewhere in the depths of her heart. She loved Nick. Clutching the bed pillows, she allowed herself the luxury of a good cry. Afterwards, feeling a bit hollow but otherwise in decent spirits, she decided she'd spent more than enough time in hiding. She left Nick's bed, grabbed her clothes from the floor, and rushed to her own room. In five minutes she was dressed in a washed-out chambray shirt and a pair of faded, soft denim jeans. Slipping her bare feet into a pair of rope sandals, she left her room.

She stood quietly at the railing looking down at the floor below, hoping to find it deserted so she could slip out of the house unnoticed.

"The coast is clear . . ." Nick's amused voice preceded him into the room. With catlike fluidity, he came across the tiled floor and stopped at the bottom of the stairs. He grinned up at her. ". . . unless you were looking for me." Laughing at her quick shake of the head, he held out his hand and invited her to join him for breakfast out on the terrace.

Rats! The last person she had wanted to see this morning was Nick. Damn him for acting as though nothing happened! she thought furiously. Unconsciously she lifted her chin and sniffed with disdain. If he could pretend that nothing had happened, so could she. With feigned indifference, she went down the stairs to him.

"Breakfast is served," he said jovially, leading her out

to the sunny terrace. He held out her chair, then slid her in and tousled her hair before bending down to give her a light kiss on the cheek. Toni shivered away from him, undecided between pretending she hated his touch and giving way to the smile that twitched on her lips.

"You're awfully chipper this morning," she said, and with a hand visibly shaking, she smoothed down her hair.

Nick laughed. "Why shouldn't I be? The sun is out, it's a beautiful day. . . . A brand new start, Toni, always gives me a good feeling."

There was something else, Toni suspected, but she knew that he would not tell her what it was until he felt like it. She glared across the table at him, thinking that he was just like Catherine when it came to being close-mouthed. And both of them possessed an unbelievable knack for pushing aside any unpleasantness, when it was convenient for *them*.

Toni quietly sipped her coffee, idly watching his hands as he filled her plate with an egg-and-cheese mixture, then spooned on a generous amount of red sauce. He was smiling rather slyly, she thought, but she charged it to his peculiar mood. She tightened her jaw and concentrated on drinking her coffee. There was no sense in showing her anger to this man; he would simply brush it aside and continue being maddeningly cheerful.

"This will clear away all the cobwebs," he said pleasantly, as he added a final splash of sauce to her plate. "Just what you need to get that awful cottony feeling out of your mouth after a binge, my poor little rich girl." He chuckled with great relish. "You're a sly little witch, you know that? I found out last night that you're hardly the poor little country girl you were pretending to be."

"I wasn't pretending anything, Nick," she contradicted in a harsh whisper. "I merely did not correct the impression you so hastily formed of me."

"I'm not trying to pry, Toni, for it's really none of my business, but just how did you manage to become so extravagantly wealthy?"

For a moment Toni considered telling him that he was right and it *was* none of his business. But she merely said, "I was born into it, Nick, same as you."

Both Nick's amusement and the smile that had so easily curved his lips disappeared with lightning swiftness. "I was not just born into it, Toni. I've had to claw my way to where I am today as though my name weren't Caldwell at all!"

Toni's dark eyebrows lifted in surprise at the bitterness she heard in his tone, but she made no comment. She knew, from Catherine, that he had started working summers for his grandfather at sixteen, in the firm's mail room, and had not been promoted to a position of any responsibility until after he had come home from college. His father was the company president at that time, and Nick had had to be satisfied with managing the steel plant's sales department when he had evidently had his heart set on running Caldwell Shipping.

She took a forkful of the spicy concoction on her plate, not noticing Nick's wicked grin until it was too late. As the fiery mixture made contact with her tongue and throat, hot tears sprang to her eyes, then ran down her tanned cheeks. She fumbled with the things in front of her, aiming for the water goblet, her entire mouth on fire.

"Serves you right," Nick said unsympathetically, slapping a piece of bread into her hand. "Here, eat this. It will absorb most of the sting." While Toni wildly stuffed the crusty bread into her scalded mouth, he poured a glass of water. Grinning impishly, he held it out to her.

Grabbing it, Toni chug-a-lugged the water.

"Told you it would clear away the cobwebs," Nick teased, eyes watery from laughing. "Now, give—" He threw her a snowy piece of linen. "Here, use this."

Toni glared at his unrepentant expression. He had known what that miserable concoction would do to her, and he had enjoyed every minute of her discomfort to the fullest. She blew her nose noisily, then leaned her elbows on the table, propping her chin on her interlaced fingers to make her glare felt. Nick smiled, unperturbed.

"I don't mean to pry, Toni, honest," he said, his indestructible smile curving his lips and playing havoc with her already agitated pulse. "I'm just curious, that's all." He took a sip of his water, then set his glass down and started to toy with it, moving it around in circles. "It's just that I know you could not have gotten a dime from Cath—your aunt." There was an unpleasant curl to his mouth as he stumbled over her mother's name. He sighed deeply, then lifted his eyes to her face.

"She's not my aunt, Nick, she's my mother," Toni informed him quietly. If only Catherine could accept that fact, it would be so much easier for Toni to admit that she loved her mother, despite her many and extravagant foibles. But Catherine could never face reality. Acknowledging the existence of a twenty-five-year-old daughter would make her considerably older than the thirty-six years she usually claimed to be.

Nick did not even blink at her confession. His features were impassive, his smile fixed; the bland expression in his eyes made her think of unpolished emeralds.

Slowly, his gaze dropped to his plate, and without a word, he began to eat as though having his breakfast was the only important thing in the entire world.

At last, he pushed his plate aside and took out a cigarette. He leaned back in his chair to enjoy his smoke, giving the impression that their conversation, as well as their breakfast, was at an end. Toni got up to leave.

"Don't go, Toni."

Startled, she stared at him, then shrugged and resumed her seat. She had nothing better to do, after all, and she thought she was carrying herself off pretty well, considering. Nick was none the wiser about the secret longing deep in her heart.

"About those accounts of yours, Toni, I——"

"If you must know, Nick, I inherited from Grandfather MacGregor," she said frigidly. She stood up abruptly, and went across to the railing, fighting against remembering why it had been she and not her father or mother who had inherited the MacGregor Mills. But she remembered anyway. Her grandfather hated Catherine and had disinherited his only son Jamie as punishment for having married her. Toni knew that her mother was impossible—like a petulant child, really—but she was still overwhelmed with aching sadness when she realized that others had come to hate her. It was as if Toni herself were being rejected.

Eyes misting with remembered hurt were cast downward to the green and foam-flecked sea lapping gently to shore. The movement of the water mesmerized her, and she did not hear Nick leave the table and come to her.

"And it doesn't make you happy that he loved you so much that he left you everything he had?" Nick's hands took gentle hold of her shoulders, but Toni escaped them and moved a few steps away.

"No." She shook her head. "It wasn't love that prompted him to make me his heir," she said. "He was a crotchety old man who forgave me for being Catherine's child, *and* female, and endowed me with his wealth only because at a very early age I discovered his Achilles heel. I learned to play every kind of game he liked, and perfected it just to be be able to beat him at it." She smiled, remembering how James Murdoch MacGregor would pound his cane on the marble floor of his study in frustration because she could checkmate him easily when she was ten.

Smiling, Nick moved closer to her. "Good at games, are you?" he asked suavely, his meaning expressed only too clearly by the hands that were suddenly roaming with wicked intent over her body.

Toni gritted her teeth and tried to shake off those tantalizing hands, but without success.

"I learn easily, Nick," she said coldly, "and once I learn them, I never forget the rules, no matter who makes them." She slid away from his marauding hands and turned to go, only to be pulled to a stop by his hand closing around her arm.

"Don't go, Toni." His large hands closed over her upper arms, and he turned her around to face him. "Come on, honey, smile. I promise you, it won't cause wrinkles."

Toni felt confused by this mood of his, and in the next moment he added to her confusion by taking her gently in his arms. She lifted her head, started to protest, and his mouth closed down over hers, his arms imprisoning her against his hard, virile frame as he kissed her with sweet and tender insistence. At first Toni tried to break away, but his strong arms tightened again. Thinking she would like to kick him for behaving like a fourteen-carat cad one minute and then doing this, Toni forced herself to stand rigidly in his arms, giving him neither the satisfaction of complete surrender nor the opportunity to show her the full extent of his strength.

"Come on, honey, smile," he said as he held her away from him. He lifted a hand and lightly ran a finger over the outline of her tightened jaw, his eyes roaming over her angry expression, finally coming to rest on her pursed lips.

His mouth curved in a charming smile meant to coax a responsive smile from her. "I don't know how to apologize, Toni...I've never had to before. When I found out that you and Catherine were related, I felt like I'd been kicked in the stomach and robbed. You were my special discovery, sweetheart, and I romanticized the idea that you were poor and alone in the world, that you had nothing to do with the cynical and worldly set of people I've come to know and despise." Nick's hand drifted across Toni's shoulder and down to her clenched fist. Gently, he uncurled each finger and took her hand firmly in his own. "Of course, now that I've had a chance to think things over, perhaps it is better that you are independently wealthy. That way neither of us has to wonder what hidden role money may play in keeping us together. Anyway, what I'm trying to say is that I took out my anger and hurt on you last night—or rather, early this morning—and I'm sorry." His hand cupped her chin, lifting her face to his.

"I want us to stay together, really I do. Can we please start again, Toni, from today?"

Toni's eyes widened in surprise. This was coming a long way down from the heights of his arrogance, she thought. She opened her mouth to tell him she did not want to play this nerve-jangling game anymore, but the hopeful expression in his eyes softened her heart. She loved him. And there was nothing she would like better than to forget every bad thing that had passed between them.

"All right, Nick. We'll start again from today." She smiled tremulously. He let out his breath in a sigh of relief, and before she could move out of his arms, he bent his head and kissed her hard and fast. Toni's lips tingled from his touch, and he bent down to kiss her again, this time with slow deliberation.

Toni knew if she let him continue, she would never want him to stop. But she was still afraid. For a moment, during Nick's apology, she had felt that he was serious about the marriage, but he was so unpredictable. She had no way of knowing what mood he'd be in a few hours from now. Toni summoned all her resolve and broke away from Nick's embrace, whispering hoarsely, "I'm still shaken up from last night, Nick, and I need a little more time." For a moment his grip tightened on her shoulders before releasing her as she added in a small voice, "Please." Toni then walked back into the house, leaving Nick on the terrace, a rueful expression on his handsome face.

Through most of the day Toni managed to avoid being alone with Nick. The last thing in this world that she wanted was to give him another opportunity to take her in his arms and attempt to seduce her. She knew now that it would no longer be a playful attempt, nor was she certain that she would have the strength of will to resist him.

Having been promised an outing that evening to a little café in a very romantic cellar where, as Nick described it, "You'll feel like you're at a clandestine rendezvous," Toni chose a long flowing gown of pink shantung with a low-cut bodice and bare back. She was in the process of donning it when Nick came into her room.

"You could at least knock," Toni protested, clutching the gown to her breast.

Looking past her, he curtly informed her that they were leaving the island immediately. His plane was fueled and ready in Palma, and his crew needed only a call from him to be on board.

"But why, Nick?"

"There are things waiting for me that can't be put off any longer," he replied crisply. Turning smartly on his heel, he strode to the door. There was a distinct droop in his shoulders, but Toni was too angry to dwell on it.

"But you promised me a vacation of three weeks, Nick, and I don't want to leave yet!" Her chin jutted out stubbornly. "I want to go to that restaurant you keep talking about, and I want to see the cathedral in Palma, and you said you would take me to—"

Nick's hands crushed a manila envelope he had carried up with him, and it seemed that his whole body tensed with anger. In a voice she thought he reserved for dealing diplomatically with unruly clients, he explained that he was a businessman with a demanding business waiting for him at home.

In her mind, Toni filled in the blanks in his explanation. He had taken three weeks to take his bride on a honeymoon, but as the bride had proved uncooperative. . . . A wild look came into her eyes as she debated whether to argue with him or start crying.

"All right, Nick," she breathed resignedly. She flung down the gown, and bent to pick up her jeans and blouse from the floor.

Nick's sharp intake of breath should have warned her, but she was too preoccupied with her own miserable thoughts to worry about him. She stood rigidly while Nick's arms went around her bent form. There was nothing to ward off the scorching fire of his touch, nor did she possess the strength or will to fight the desire that his hands on her body immediately aroused. She shivered with longing as he very gently lifted her, at the same time turning her around in his arms. The jeans and blouse dropped slowly from her nerveless fingers, and she turned her face to his in expectation.

"Lord," Nick murmured thickly, "you either really don't know what you do to me or you don't care." With a groan, he lowered his head and crushed her mouth. His arms closed around her body with fierce, bruising intensity. Her head swam, and she tried to pull away, desperately needing a breath of head-clearing air. But he curled his long hard fingers into her hair and held her head while he took what he wanted from her trembling mouth.

Moments went by, long moments when Toni felt she would die of the exquisite pleasure he was giving her with his hands traveling at will over her back, caressing, exploring, teasing until she felt like screaming. He found the hook-and-eye closing of her strapless bra and quickly undid it.

A moan escaped their merging mouths as he moved slightly to let the flimsy garment fall to the floor between them.

"Toni . . ." His breath was a soft caress against her

lips. He murmured her name again and again while trailing light nibbling kisses down the column of her neck and across her shoulder.

The bed loomed within the periphery of Toni's vision. Dimly, she realized she was now cradled in Nick's powerful arms and he was moving toward the bed. She put up a token struggle.

"Don't push me away, honey," he begged against her throat. His breath brushed warmly over her skin. "I want you, baby, I want you."

Into her confused thoughts sprang the warning she had received from Catherine. Nick Caldwell had no heart; he took and took, never giving in return. To him, then, she was only a new diversion.

"No, Nick!" she managed hoarsely. Laughing huskily, Nick ignored her words, moving his mouth down over the throbbing pulse at the base of her throat and on down to soft breasts.

She moaned softly as Nick, his tongue still teasing one pink nipple into tautness, lowered her gently to the bed. He did not stop his gentle seduction even as he tore open his silk shirt.

"Don't be frightened, sweetheart, I promise I'll be gentle."

Toni caught a patch of blue out of the corner of her eye as Nick flung his shirt away. His dark blue slacks followed.

A lazy, dangerous languidity flowed through her limbs as he lay down beside her. Breathlessly, she pleaded, "Oh, please, Nick, let me go!"

"No," he rasped out, his mouth settling with maddening slowness on one breast.

Toni was lost! "Nick..." Slowly, her arms found

their way around his neck, her fingers eagerly tangled themselves in the mass of curling black hair at the nape.

"That's much better, baby," he approved, sighing with satisfaction.

Toni was on fire. There was no more fight left in her; she wanted what was happening. Lifting her face up for his kiss, she told herself that even if he did not love her, she loved him, and that would be enough ... for now.

"Toni," he murmured sweetly against her lips as he prepared to take more than just kisses from her.

An insistent rapping at the door interrupted the merging of their bodies.

Nick swore. "What is it?" he snarled, glaring at the unseen person at the door.

"Oh!" After a long pause, Maria said in a voice choked with embarrassment, "Forgive me, *señora, señora,* for the interruption ..."

Stifling Nick's volley of sharp-edged curses with a hand pressed to his mouth, Toni urged Maria to tell her what she wanted.

"A lady is here to see *Señor* Caldwell," Maria said swiftly, albeit nervously. "She says she must speak with him, it is urgent."

A lady? Toni doubted that. Urgent? I just bet it is, she thought bitterly. "What's her name, Maria?" she asked unhappily, knowing who was asking for Nick even before the embarrassed maid told them it was Nancy Kincaid.

Nick stiffened. Veiling her own unhappiness with an indifference she was far from feeling, Toni pushed him away from her and rolled over to the other side of the bed.

"You'd better go to her, Nick," she muttered, pushing

away the hands that reached for her. She wanted to scream at him, to beat her fists against his hairy chest, claw his face, hurt him as much as she was hurting inside. "You don't want to keep her waiting." Closing her eyes against the searing pain in her breast, she sniffed to keep the tears welling in her eyes from spilling over.

"I don't want to go, you know that, don't you?" Nick whispered in her ear, lightly biting her lobe, driving her crazy with desire.

"Do I, Nick?" she demanded tersely.

"You should, Toni," he replied softly, then his warm, firm lips came down to hers again and his fingers nimbly, teasingly, explored the most private regions of her body, making her cringe with shame as her body began to arch toward him in response.

A pulse beat erratically at her throat, and it was there that Nick settled his mouth. Toni fought hard to push him away, but Nick would not move. She felt herself flushing hotly when Nick purposely pressed his hips against her to make her aware of his arousal.

"I hope this convinces you how very much I want to stay," he said, smiling wickedly. Then he locked her eyes in a steady gaze. "Ask me not to go, Toni."

Toni refused to take up his challenge even though what she wanted most in life was to keep him from going to Nancy. But she would not say the words. If he stayed, it would have to be because *he* wanted to.

Nick maintained his forbidding expression a moment longer, then he grinned. "You damned little feisty kitten," he teased, stealing a kiss from her unsmiling lips. Then he added, "I won't be long, so don't lose my place," as he rolled away from her and left the bed.

Toni tightened her jaw, furiously. Don't hurry on my account, she told him silently, eyes bright with anger fixed on him as he climbed back into his clothes. If Nancy had anything to say about it, Toni would be lucky to see him before tomorrow.

As soon as the door had closed behind him, Toni turned her face to the pillow and allowed her tears to fall. "Oh, Nick, I love you," she cried brokenly, beating the pillow with her clenched fists. But it was clear he preferred being with Nancy, even when she was on the verge of giving herself to him. Maybe he loved Nancy, Toni thought bitterly, though why he had not married her, she could not even guess.

CHAPTER SIX

TONI CAUTIOUSLY SHIFTED positions in her seat, trying not to touch Nick sitting beside her on the matching honey velvet high-backed seat. Very carefully she reached across to the pocket on the wall of the cabin and flipped through the magazines there, desperately trying to keep herself from thinking about the horrible scene she had witnessed late last night in the courtyard of their villa. But nothing would chase the memory from her mind.

She could still see Nick leaning against the car fender, illuminated by a traitorous silver moon, a cigarette dangling negligently from the corner of his mouth. He spoke to Nancy in a low whisper, and for a moment Toni was convinced that their association was all as Nick claimed—purely business. But then Nancy closed the distance between them, arching her voluptuous body toward Nick.

Toni could not stand any more and had let the drapes
fall over the window.

"Toni?"

Nick's voice intruded into her thoughts, bringing her
quickly back into the present. She turned to him with a
blank expression in her eyes, the unread magazine still
in her hands.

"Toni, you've been ignoring me all day, and I know
you're angry because of last night, but honestly, it was
just business with Nancy last night."

"You don't have to explain anything to me, Nick,"
she said in a tone of dismissal, resuming her perusal of
the magazine.

Suddenly the magazine was jerked away and Toni was
left with her hands curled around nothing. Angrily, she
twisted around in her seat, prepared to do battle, but
Nick warned her quietly to listen to him.

"You are entitled to an explanation, and you are going
to get one even if it kills you," he muttered. His expression told her that if what he had to say did not put things
right between them, it would not be for lack of trying
on his part.

"Nancy's ex-husband owns a small block of stocks
that I want, but they are tied up in a computer servicing
business that's going downhill fast. As she is still half-
owner, Nancy is doing all she can to promote the sale
of the business to Caldwell Industries. But I want to buy
it myself, out of my own pocket." He paused to take a
breath, and Toni turned to look out the window as the
Caldwell plane took a dip over the Atlantic. She selected
another magazine.

"It means a lot to me, Toni, if you'll say you believe
me."

She did not, but what did it matter? It cost her a brief moment of discomfort to give him the answer he wanted, but Nick was not satisfied.

"You have a very suspicious nature, Toni," he gritted through clenched teeth, his tone weary and frustrated.

Toni shrugged. "If you say so."

She heard him muttering beside her, and then the second magazine was wrested from her hands. Toni firmly clasped her hands together on her lap and turned to view the cloudy scene outside her window.

"Toni, turn around and look at me!"

Harshly spoken, the words were a command she knew she dared not disobey. Her jaw tightening, she turned and snapped, "What is it, Nick—another apology?"

To her surprise Nick looked slightly shamefaced. "No, Toni. I believe I've apologized enough for one day." He took her hands and began to play with her wedding ring. Catching the light from the lamps overhead, the emerald glittered as brightly as Nick's eyes as they contemplated the hand that trembled in his.

"Toni, let's start again? Let's pretend that we've just met, and take it from there?" Round and round he twisted her ring as he spoke, until it began to feel like a branding iron on her skin, hot and bruising. Wincing, Toni tried to withdraw her hand from his.

"Don't pull away from me, Toni!" he ordered sharply.

"This isn't getting us anywhere, Nick," she retorted, tugging impatiently at her hand, more than a little annoyed with herself for enjoying the warmth of his touch.

He leaned toward her, and for one breathtaking moment she thought he would kiss her. Sucking in a quick breath, she pulled back, away from the lips she felt a frightening urge to devour. Her heart began an erratic thudding against her chest, restricting her breathing.

"What do you want from me, Nick?" she whispered hoarsely, her eyes riveted to the hand imprisoned in his.

A stifled noise that vaguely resembled a laugh erupted from his throat. "Oh, Toni, if you only knew!" He began to play with her ring again. "What I want, honey . . . what I *really* want—" The frigid expression in her eyes stopped him, and he smiled ruefully. "Can't we at least be *friends*, Toni?"

"Whatever you want, Nick," she returned dully. She turned away so that he would not see the tears glistening in her eyes.

What she would not give to hear him say instead, "I love you, Toni."

She sighed wistfully as, without another word, Nick left his seat and went forward to the cockpit.

The plane set down smoothly at San Francisco International. Nick shook Toni awake and told her that she was home.

"Home?" she repeated drowsily.

"Well, almost home," he amended. "Your new home is still a few minutes away, in the Berkeley Hills."

Toni gathered her purse and the carryall she always took with her when flying. Out of the corner of her eye, she saw Nick glancing at his watch, and she wondered if he had a business appointment somewhere, so soon. She frowned. The idea of being left alone in a strange house was about as appealing to her as dirty dishwater. She glanced up at his face, wondering if she dared to suggest that she wait while he took care of business, and found Nick looking down at her. She was startled by the intensity of his gaze and the way his eyes seemed to devour every inch of her, from her feathered black hair to her sandaled feet.

"How about a drink before starting for home, Toni?" He reached down to take her carryall from her. "That way we'll miss the commuter traffic," he added softly.

"That would be nice, Nick. Thank you for suggesting it." At least this showed he didn't want to get away from her.

"My pleasure." He smiled. Toni felt an unaccountable warmth spread through her lower limbs and looked hastily away.

Nick took her hand as they went down the ramp to solid ground, then he loosely draped an arm across her shoulders as they headed for the airport lounge.

While they waited for their drinks, Nick told her about the Caldwell house in the Berkeley Hills. It had been left to him by his grandfather, but he had not lived in it since his grandmother had died several summers before. It was too big for just him, he claimed, adding that he had an apartment in San Francisco that was close to his office and satisfied all his needs. He paused and glanced up at the waitress as she set down their drinks.

"Or it did," he amended softly the moment the woman left them. His large hand curled around his glass, and for a moment he just stared into the ice floating in the Scotch.

Toni toyed with her glass of wine, taking small sips while thoughts whirled with dizzying speed through her fertile brain, hurling her to that mysterious house Nick had described.

"The staff goes home at night, Toni; I hope you don't mind that." His voice, stiff and formal, was like a pin popping a child's balloon.

Toni's mind left a dream in which the house in Berkeley was her and Nick's little love nest, and lifted her gaze to meet his. "No, of course not, Nick. I'm used to looking after myself. I prefer it, in fact."

An odd expression flitted across his features. Toni figured it was because he wanted her to say that she could not cope on her own. Oh, if he only knew how often she'd been on her own!

"I'll get you settled in, Toni, and tomorrow you'll be on your own. I have to go to Los Angeles on business. I'll probably be gone two, maybe three days."

Toni blinked. He had plucked her out of New Orleans, where she had been quite comfortable and happy. And now he had the colossal nerve to plant her in a strange house and then leave!

"If you're done with your drink . . . ?" Nick pushed back his chair and stood up.

"I know that Mrs. Mansfield—the housekeeper, sort of—stocked the pantry and the fridge, so you're well taken care of in the food department. If there's anything else you think you'll need while I'm gone, please tell me."

Toni's lips compressed into a hard, unfriendly line, and Nick's smile faded with lightning swiftness.

"What's wrong, Toni?" She heard honest concern in his voice and quickly glanced up in surprise. She found a soft, almost tender expression on his face that both surprised and confused her.

Pride urged her to deny that there was anything wrong, but she so wanted him to ask her to go with him that she braved saying, "It's only that I didn't expect to be deserted the minute we arrived in California, Nick."

Perhaps it was her use of the word *deserted,* or perhaps

it was the fact that Nick was already feeling guilty about leaving her alone that made him suddenly angry, but he replied in a fierce whisper, "You knew what it was going to be like, Toni, when you accepted my proposition.

"After all," he added caustically, "it's not as if ours were a real marriage where I would feel obligated to ask you to go wherever I go."

Toni smiled frigidly. So much for her silly dreams, she thought sadly, and pretended interest in looking for Nick's car to avoid the hand that was being suddenly offered to her.

The next day, Toni awoke to find the house deserted. She stared across the terrace railing to the city in miniature that was San Francisco and reflected on the events that had brought her to this lush estate. Her first view of the Caldwell home had been from the window of Nick's red Maserati as they wound their way up Old Tunnel Road. Nestled among tall trees, the Caldwell home sprawled in several levels over one of the most scenic of the East Bay hills. The architect had made a most dramatic use of the natural elements, tastefully combining them with a conventional charm and elegance that took her breath away—enhancing, rather than detracting from, the beauty of the landscape.

It seemed the perfect setting for playboy Nick, but it was not home for her. After living with Fannie. and finding in that little house in New Orleans the only warmth and happiness she had ever known, Toni found the Caldwell mansion too grand to evoke anything but unease, especially now that she was alone.

Why hadn't Nick taken her with him? With a sudden pang of jealousy she thought that perhaps Nancy Kincaid had—unexpectedly of course!—decided to return home too. After all, Toni had read that she, too, lived in San Francisco. She cringed under the furious assault of her emotions.

Rather than remain idle and allow her thoughts to torture her further, she went back into the house. Now that she had time, she might as well start studying for her law boards.

Upstairs in her room, with its panoramic view of the bay, she knelt beside her trunk, which had arrived from New Orleans, and loaded her arms with her thick, dusty law tomes. Nearly staggering under their weight, she retraced her steps to Nick's study on the second level of the big house and sat down in his desk chair. With Nick's things all around her, perhaps she wouldn't feel so lonely.

Opening one of the books, Toni became quickly involved in the intricacies of the law that she so loved, and for an hour she was happy. Then she looked up and began searching for a pad to make notes. Poking through the clutter on Nick's desk, she found a newspaper announcement of their marriage, probably put there by the housekeeper. Then a large wrinkled manila envelope caught her eye. Toni's mind flashed back to the moment when Nick had burst into her room on their last day in Majorca, grasping a crumpled envelope in his hand. Impulsively, she opened it and gasped when she found herself staring down into her own face. Flanking her at either side in the eight-by-ten glossy, which now shook in her hand, were two of the young men she had met at Margarita Fuentes' party. As she remembered, the two had been trying to teach her a silly little dance they had invented. A rather innocent pose, taken at face value, but the caption at the bottom of the picture was another matter.

> The country mouse plays while the cat paying
> all the bills is doing *what*, Nicky?

was written in bright red ink in a distinctively feminine hand.

Toni closed her eyes tightly. It all slowly fell into place. She smiled ruefully. Why, Nick must have been jealous! It was no wonder he had plucked her out of there so fast!

Leaving things exactly as she had found them, Toni gathered her books and swiftly departed from Nick's study, fully convinced that had it not been for that blasted picture, Nick would not have suddenly recalled pressing business in California. Vowing silently that the minute Nick came home she would clear the air and tell him that the picture meant nothing, she went up to her room and stretched out on her bed to read. Yet even the fascination law held for her could not keep her awake now, and she fell asleep with a smile, knowing that Nick must care for her more than he would admit.

Toni awoke the next morning to find dappled sunlight filtering into her room. For a moment she lay very still, her thoughts disorganized, her grey green eyes roaming over her unfamiliar surroundings. She was in a generously sized room with French doors that opened out to her own porticoed redwood balcony. On one wall stood an old fashioned oak dresser topped with a huge mirror. Opposite was a chaise longue of rose beige velvet, and

on it occasional pillows of knobby linen. She had slept
upon a heavy four-poster bed covered with a bedspread
that matched the hue and fabric of the chaise. The carpet
was patterned, employing all the colors that had been so
painstakingly selected to give the room a charming, rest-
ful appeal. Twin ceramic lamps stood on matching night-
stands at either side of the bed to complete the room's
furnishings.

She remembered where she was and smiled, pleased
with her new room. She recalled Nick telling her that his
grandmother had decorated and occupied this room.

Stretching lazily, she yawned, then flung off her covers and reluctantly rolled out of bed. She stepped out
into the fresh morning air, delighting in the view of the
bay and San Francisco in the distance.

Below her lay the goldfish pond, which Nick had told
her his grandfather had personally built to accommodate
the bucketful of goldfish a seven-year-old Nick had won
at a school carnival. The fish had not remained long,
thanks to a prowling, hungry cat, but the memory would
never die for Nick.

Toying with images of her husband as a little boy,
Toni slipped back into her room. Nick had called last
night to say he was coming home today. The thought
thrilled her as much as hearing his voice had. She smiled,
and went into the bathroom that separated her room from
Nick's.

Brass fixtures, black marble sink and sunken bathtub,
massager showerhead, Jacuzzi—Toni grinned, thinking
Nick's grandmother could not be held responsible for
decorating the bathroom. Turning on both faucets full
blast over the tub, Toni wiggled out of her nightgown
and, dousing the water liberally with bath oil, she stepped

into her bath. Her flesh tingled pleasurably as she immersed herself up to her chin.

Smiling, she left her bath, toweled herself off, and stepped back into her room. Her smile widened as she donned a bathrobe. She had plenty of time to dash back up to her room to throw on something appropriate for Nick's homecoming, but for now she was dying for a cup of coffee.

Unexpectedly she collided with Nick as she was entering the kitchen. He grasped her shoulders with both hands to steady her, in the process dropping the cup of coffee he had been carrying to the breakfast nook just off the kitchen.

"Oh, Toni, I hope I didn't burn you," he said, swinging her away from the broken china cup and spilled coffee on the tiled floor.

Oh, but he had! she thought, shivering with the sweet pain caused by his fiery touch.

"Did you miss me, Toni?" he murmured, drawing her to him.

Yes! cried Toni's quickening heart, but instead she said lightly, "You weren't gone long enough to be missed. Now would you please let me go so that I can get a cup of coffee?"

Nick frowned. "But what about the mess on the floor, Toni? Aren't you going to clean it up?"

"*I* didn't break the cup." Extremely conscious of her less than appealing attire, she shook herself free of him, stepped over the mess, and hurried into the kitchen.

"Why the heck do I have a wife, then...?" came Nick's voice, half amused, half reproachful.

"I don't know, Nick," she retorted, coming to a stop at the doorway. She held her cup so that the steam rising from the hot coffee went up to her face and lightly veiled her hopeful expression. "Why *did* you marry me, Nick?"

Nick's lips curved in a crooked, roguish grin, and his eyes glittered with wicked purpose. "Why don't we go up to my bedroom and I'll show you, Toni," he said silkily, advancing toward her.

Realizing suddenly that Nick knew she was naked under the robe, Toni took a step back. Her hands shook as she took the cup to her lips, forcing herself to drink the hot liquid. A swift, soothing warmth flowed through her that restored her equilibrium. She managed a little smile despite the quivering of her lips.

"Why don't you take me out to breakfast instead, Nick?" she asked, and with a hand visibly shaking, she set her cup down on the small round table in the breakfast nook.

"Coward!" he hissed, laughing merrily as Toni started to cross in front of him. He sent out his arms to block her escape, but Toni went under them and away.

If the staff were on hand, Nick would not be so outrageously flirtatious, she told herself as she hurried into her room to dress. Still . . . his playful attempts at seduction were good for her ego.

We could have planned this, she thought amusedly a few moments later when she saw Nick coming through the bathroom and into her room. Nick, casual but immaculate in tan slacks and a short-sleeved shirt of a coral hue, came striding across the thick carpet, his green eyes taking in her svelte form. She wore a sleeveless silk blouse of pale orange over butter-soft camel slacks.

"I'm almost ready," she whispered, grabbing her comb.

"You look good enough to eat, Toni. Are you sure

you wouldn't rather stay here for a light breakfast, and
then . . . ?" He inclined his head meaningfully, giving her
a smile that made her heart flutter wildly.

"Are you trying to weasel out of buying me breakfast?" she demanded, looking away from him to hide the
becoming blush tinting her cheeks. "I assure you, I am
no cook!"

Nick chuckled. "Neither am I, so I guess we'd better
go out." Cupping his hand under her elbow, he pulled
her close. He bent down and kissed her, with deliberate
slowness.

"You're not always going to be able to put me off,
Toni," he warned her softly, releasing her. "But for now,
let's go feed you." Laughing huskily at the stricken look
on her face, he took her brush, threw it on her dresser,
then took her by the arm and ushered her out of the room.

Three little words, that's all it would take, and he'd
have her in his bed so fast it would make his head spin!
But *I love you* was probably not even in her husband's
vocabulary, she realized, and sighed imperceptibly as
she accompanied him out into the brisk morning air.

CHAPTER SEVEN

"WHERE ARE WE going now, Nick?" Toni asked as he helped her into his sleek red Maserati. Leaning her head back, she now regretted she had not followed her first instinct: to order a child's portion of whatever Nick suggested.

"Home, Toni, where, if things worked out the way I planned them, you'll have a surprise waiting for you." His grin was wide, somewhat teasing.

"A surprise?" Eyes glittering with curiosity, Toni turned to face him, her lips curved in a smile. She loved surprises. "What kind of surprise, Nick?"

"Wait and see." His tone was amused.

"I can't, Nick!" She tugged on his pantleg. "Tell me now!" But he shook his head, grinning wickedly, and quietly asked her to watch what she was doing with his thigh. Toni blushed and pulled herself stiffly against the window, hating herself for feeling so trembly inside. She forced her attention to the scenery outside her window.

"Not that I mind, Toni," Nick teased. "It's rather pleasant, in fact. It's just that at the moment I am in no position to return the favor, or take you up on your veiled invitation."

Toni sniffed. That comment did not deserve a reply.

He laughed, and her heart jerked involuntarily.

"You're impossible, Nick Caldwell! Is *that* all a man like you has on his mind?" And before he could answer, she added, smugly, "I know, it's a car!" recalling he had promised to give her one.

"Now you went and blew the big surprise," he chided.

"But I didn't guess what kind of car it is, Nick, or the color," she apologized sweetly.

"It's silver, babe, to match your wedding ring," he teased. "A Jaguar," he added, sighing with mock regret. "There, I hope you're satisfied now that your surprise is ruined, brat!"

A Jaguar! Toni was mortified! A wave of apprehension washed over her. "You might as well have let me drive this one," she muttered ungraciously, thinking of the long nose on the Jaguar that Bob Carlson drove.

"If you value your neck, Toni Caldwell, you'll never try to drive my Maser."

Toni's head jerked up with surprise at the deadly calm and possessive quality of his voice. She wondered if he was always so jealous of what he owned.

Coolly calculating eyes were lifted to his face. "Are you this possessive with everything?" she queried softly.

"Only with what's mine, Toni," he returned just as quietly, and promptly changed the subject.

"Tomorrow I have to fly down to Mexico, to close

a deal for Caldwell Shipping. I don't know how long I'll be gone, Toni, but I hope you won't be too . . . lonely."

Was there a hint of mockery in his tone? she wondered. He had never even mentioned that picture of her with the two men at Margarita's soiree, but was that what he was thinking of right now?

It was now or never. She opened her mouth to explain about the misleading photograph of her at the Fuentes party, then closed it again. A kind of paralysis settled over her and the conciliatory words simply would not come. Finally, she managed to say, "Don't worry about me, Nick, I'm used to being alone. It will give me a chance to do some solid studying."

His thick eyebrows gathered in a scowl, and for a moment Toni thought he was going to throw that miserable episode up at her. Then he muttered something about bringing her a gift from Mexico and said nothing more until they were facing their own driveway.

It was empty.

"I guess the delivery of your car is going to be delayed, Toni. I'm sorry."

Toni was not. She was so relieved, she could have kissed whoever was holding it up. "Oh, don't be, Nick, it's all right," she assured him with a soft, airy laugh. Smiling, she reached out and touched his arm. "Come on. You need to pack."

Nick touched the hand on his arm, briefly, but the glow of warmth that had started into his eyes suddenly chilled to cold, flat hardness. "Yes, I do, don't I?" he said tonelessly, and shifted the car into gear to take it up the rest of the way.

Wordlessly, he lifted himself out of his bucket seat and hurried around the car to open her door. Toni's eyes narrowed in concern when he yanked her out of the car and hurried her across the courtyard to the house.

She was skimming over the ground, and his fingers were digging into the fleshy part of her upper arm. "Nick, hold up a bit!" she cried in vexation. He opened the door and pulled her into the house. "Good God, Nick, there's no need to run," she muttered, breaking free of the painful grip he had on her arm.

"Yes, there is, Toni," he contradicted in a harsh whisper. "You see, I'm just like you—I don't stay where I'm not wanted." Pivoting on his heel, he strode swiftly away. Bewildered, Toni watched him take the stairs by twos, visibly wincing when she heard him slam the door of his bedroom. The sound reverberated throughout the empty house.

Perhaps she had hurt him with her lack of enthusiasm over his gift. Perhaps if she went up and told him how she felt about driving such a big car. Determined to apologize, Toni started up the stairs, only to stop when she heard Nick on the extension phone in the hall. Should she wait until he was through talking . . . or should she go up and let him know that she was there?

"I don't care what you have to offer her!" Nick nearly shouted into the phone. "I need those stocks!"

It was only a business call, and whatever was going on in that aspect of his life was really none of her concern. Toni started to leave, but stopped when she heard Nick's laughter. Casting aside her scruples, she leaned against the wall to listen, curious to find out what had made Nick laugh after he had been so angry just a moment before.

"Look," she heard him say, quietly confident, "I told you already, Don. You can leave Nancy safely in my hands." Another low laugh erupted from him, a laugh of triumph laced with mockery.

Toni's mouth twisted convulsively. And so would she, she promised herself furiously. They deserved each other! He could turn on all the charm he possessed, but never again would she allow him to move her. Angry tears swam in her eyes, slipping out of the corners and dripping down her cheeks, but Toni would not give in to them. Swallowing them hastily back, she pushed away from the wall and ran quietly down the stairs.

Leave Nancy safely in his hands! she thought venomously as she wound her way through the beauty of the garden to her favorite spot under the aged apple tree. No doubt he would try to convince her that *that* was business, too!

Dropping down on the grass, she leaned her back against the bark of the tree and closed her eyes in pain. Fannie had warned her repeatedly that curiosity brought unwelcome and sometimes painful revelations, but she would never learn. Oh, why had she not stayed downstairs? Then, at least, she would not have known that the Kincaid woman was still very much in the picture.

She forced her mind to other things, and soon her eyelids grew heavy. She did not fight the sleep that descended upon her. She had no intention of spending time with Nick when his mind was on Nancy Kincaid.

A wind that rustled the leaves overhead woke her. Slowly, she rose and trudged dejectedly back to the house.

Nick was gone. The silence in the house taunted her with the message even before she went up to her room and found his note pinned to her pillow.

"Something" had come up. . . . He had had to leave sooner that he had expected. . . . There was a brief mention of the fact that her car had arrived, but Toni was in no mood to look at it.

Donning dungarees and a white knit shirt, Toni grabbed her law books and went down to Nick's study. She was serious about preparing for the law boards, but deep down she also knew that this was the one room in which she felt closest to Nick. Kicking off her shoes, she dropped down on the leather couch by the window and stretched her legs over the armrest, her eyes for a moment not seeing the law text she had selected.

A memory of Nick's warm hands caressing her soft skin to erotic pleasure came to mind, a memory that was almost unbearable. She started missing him with an intensity that tied her stomach muscles in knots.

Damn him! At this rate she'd never get anything done.

The house was too large, too quiet. Even when the cook, the housekeeper, the secretary, and the gardener were somewhere around she still felt all alone.

"I know!" She dropped off the couch and went to the phone on Nick's desk. She would call Frank MacPherson, her lawyer. Maybe he could help her find work in a law firm. Before taking the exam, she'd need some practical experience, and a job would get her out of the house.

"Toni!" Frank's voice was vibrant with joy at hearing from her. He congratulated her for "hooking" the biggest catch in the country, adding that Nick was the lucky one for having found her.

"Isn't he, though?" Toni agreed with a dry laugh.

Social amenities over, Toni posed her problem to him. There was a short, somewhat surprised pause.

"So you want to return to your law career, Toni?"

"I never really considered dropping it." She paused, smiling slyly. "I thought maybe you knew someone who needs a law clerk?"

Soft laughter skimmed through the wire, lightly mocking her. "You little rascal. You were hoping I'd give you a job here, weren't you?"

Toni blushed. This man had always been able to see through her. She sighed. "Not really," she denied. "It's just that—"

"It's all right, I understand." He chuckled. "You can come in three or four days a week and help my staff if you'd like. In fact, if you're free tomorrow, you might as well come in and let me show you the ropes."

Toni agreed happily. "Great. See you in the morning, Frank. And thanks."

Jauntily, she went to her room, grabbed her purse from the foot of the bed, and left the house. If she was going to be driving to the city nearly every day, she'd better start getting used to her new car, which had been delivered while she was napping under the apple tree. Besides, she wanted to pick up some more law books in Berkeley.

Nothing ventured... Toni opened the door and slid in behind the wheel. She set the key in the ignition but did not turn it. For a moment she sat there staring out at the shiny silver hood, which seemed to stretch for miles, debating whether to risk driving the Jag or to leave it for another day when Nick would be home to supervise.

Nick would laugh at her.

That thought decided her, and she immediately turned the key and started the car.

"Piece o' cake," she bragged a few moments later,

and smiled as she nosed the car down the hill. Except for the length in front of her, driving the Jag was no different from driving Fannie's Fiat.

The next few days were enormously satisfying for Toni. Frank had assigned her to assist two of his junior partners, Dan Ramsey and a vivacious red-haired woman named Laura Jameson, who was not much older than herself. The first day Dan took her to lunch and outlined her duties. In addition to doing research—looking up precedents, county records, and so forth—she'd be given a chance to draft legal briefs and would help by taking out some of the more demanding clients for lunch or drinks. Toni was exhilarated by the chance to apply some of what she'd learned in three grueling years of law school and threw herself into the job with enthusiasm. Much to her relief, she largely succeeded in pushing Nick out of her mind.

On the third morning of her new job, Nick returned from his business trip, earlier than Toni had expected him. He was elated about something, but she did not have time to stay and listen to him. Impulsively, she lifted herself on her tiptoes and gave him a kiss on the cheek. She told him she was happy to see him, would see him again in the evening, and started out of the house before Nick could recover from his surprise.

"I'll try not to be late," she called over her shoulder.

"Where the devil are you going?" Nick demanded. His expression was grim; his eyes glinted with frustrated anger.

"I'll tell you when I get home," she said gaily.

As she eased the silver Jaguar through the narrow streets, she smiled with satisfaction.

Nick's home. Unconsciously she decreased the pressure on the accelerator and felt an almost depressing urge to turn around and go back home. But she shrugged away the feeling and forced herself to continue to the office. It would do her no good to go back. Nick would have brought his work with him and would be busy with his own affairs. Yet the urge persisted, and soon became a burning desire. But she continued onward, ignoring the longing to see Nick. Bringing all her concentration to bear on what she was doing, she pushed down on the accelerator and forced herself to think about the busy day ahead.

When she arrived home in late afternoon, looking forward to a romantic dinner with Nick, all she found was a cold note of farewell. Toni felt like crying. Nick had gone to Los Angeles for a day or two. If only she had stayed in the house long enough to hear him out, maybe he would have asked her to go with him. Unless, of course, he had already asked Nancy Kincaid! His note ended with a request that she stay at home during his absence.

The gall of the man, Toni thought bitterly. She stomped furiously into the study and opened one of her law books. With great concentration she read through two case histories on contract law. Then she burst into tears.

CHAPTER EIGHT

AFTER A SOLITARY supper, Toni took a hot bath and went to bed, but sleep eluded her. She tossed and turned, plagued by the memory of Nick's sudden departure.

Flinging off the covers, she left the bed and went out to sit on her terrace. The air was moist, cool; the moon was full, lighting the yard and adding a magical quality to the scene below. She leaned back in her redwood chaise and closed her eyes. Gradually the serenity of her surroundings soothed her, and she grew sleepy. Leaving her lounge chair, she trudged back to her bed, her eyes drooping with weariness.

She turned fitfully for the rest of the night, merely dozing, often plagued by disturbing dreams of Nick making love to Nancy Kincaid. When dawn broke she finally fell into a deep and, thankfully, dreamless sleep.

When Toni woke, feeling tired and defeated, the luminous dial on her clock read nine thirty. She threw off the covers and left the bed.

She bathed and dressed quickly in a skirt of a maroon-and-black plaid and a sleeveless maroon shell. She brushed her hair behind her ears and applied more makeup than usual to hide the dark circles under her eyes.

Toni smiled ruefully into her reflection in the mirror. She was planning to do some research in the library, then maybe take in a show before coming home. "What a way to spend my only day off this week," she murmured.

As she was descending the stairs a few minutes later, she heard a car driving up. Wondering if Nick was trying to surprise her by coming home sooner than expected, she hurried her step and rushed across the entrance hall to open the door for him, thinking to surprise *him*. She had her hand on the knob when it turned. The door opened and Nick walked in.

"Nick!" Yielding to a sudden, insane, urge to throw her arms around his neck and kiss him, she moved forward. For a fleeting moment, she saw pleasure gleaming in his eyes as his hands went out for her. But there was anger in these long, lean fingers that pressed into her shoulders. He held her away from him.

"Don't tell me you've missed me," he jeered. His eyes glittered darkly with ill-repressed anger. A pulse throbbed wildly on his tightened jaw.

Toni grimaced. The last time she'd seen that look was in Majorca, when Nick had been angered by the photograph of her and the two *caballeros*. Had Nancy been up to her tricks again?

"Where were you going when I so rudely interrupted?" he demanded, giving her a shake.

"I was going for a walk, Nick," she lied, forcing her lips to smile. It was hardly the moment to tell him about her work in the law office. She felt his fingers dig into her flesh, and winced. "Nick, you're——"

"Are you certain that's all you were going out for?" he challenged, raking her slender form insultingly. "You seem a bit overdressed for a stroll."

Toni compressed her lips in annoyance. He must think she was on her way to meet another man, and that his arrival had thrown a monkey wrench into the works! She should really give him something to worry about! she thought angrily, gritting her teeth.

"Do you really think so?" she asked, with forced calm. She took a deep breath to ease the angry pounding of her heart. "I suppose you're right. Jeans would be better than this . . ." she touched the skirt and grimaced, wishing now she had never put it on.

The wind went out of Nick's sails. "Go for your walk, Toni." His hands fell away as though he could no longer bear to touch her.

"Come with me, Nick?" she invited, wishing not only to allay his suspicions, but also to have him close to her for a few minutes before she lost him again to the work he had no doubt brought home with him. She held out her hand, a fixed smile on her lips. "Please, Nick, ignore your work for a few minutes and come with me?"

What Nick ignored was her hand. He muttered something about having several important calls to make and turned on his heel. Toni's eyes followed his tall, virile form as he crossed the room in a few stiff-legged strides. He walked, she thought sadly, as if the only thought in his mind was to put the greatest distance between them in the shortest possible time.

Slowly she went up the stairs to her room. There was no sense in being all dressed to the nines if there was no one to appreciate the way she looked.

She stood before the long, oval mirror on her closet door, morosely staring at her lovely outfit.

"Arrogant, insufferable male! I can't seem to do anything right where he's concerned!" Her lips curled downward in self-derision.

So why try? taunted a pesky little inner voice that goaded her into flinging off the skirt and blouse that had made her look so deliciously feminine. Angrily drawing on a pair of faded denims and a white blouse, she left her room and went back downstairs.

A need to be noticed was almost smothering her as she positioned herself on a chair where Nick could not fail to see her when he came out of his study. Unless, of course, he chose to ignore her completely.

Nick came out a few minutes later, a sheaf of papers in his hand, a small frown furrowing his wide brow.

"Toni, I—" He stopped, looked down at her, and chuckled. "Back in uniform, eh?" he teased, and Toni glowered at him. He shot her a mocking glance, then continued in a low, toneless voice.

"You've been a rather busy little beaver lately," he said, fanning the papers in his hand. Toni drew back, but remained silent, nibbling on her lower lip in vexation. What had happened to the surly character that had met her at the door and all but accused her of cheating on her marriage vows? Nick stood in front of her, cool and calm as though not an angry word had passed between them.

"Did you think perhaps I would not approve?"

"Approve?" she echoed in confusion.

"You weren't listening." His chiding tone added fuel to the flame smoldering inside her.

"Oh? Were you saying something?"

For a moment he appeared on the verge of losing his temper, and Toni could only marvel that she remained where she was and that the calm mask she had slipped on when he had moved her legs aside and sat down on the armrest had stayed firmly in place under his baleful glare. Nick sighed, and then continued.

"I was saying, Toni, that I would have enjoyed hearing from you that you were working for Frank MacPherson's law firm, but even if I had to learn it from other sources, I'm glad you found something useful to do with your time." He glanced around the large room, his eyes lingering briefly on the piano before moving on to touch each piece of furniture that adorned the oversized room. He shuddered slightly, as if with cold. "It must be an awful bore being here. . . ." His voice faded to a silence pregnant with remorse.

Toni stared at him, aware that in a roundabout way he was saying that he admired what she was doing, but she was also unhappy because he had not said he would take her with him on his trips to keep her from being bored.

Toni smiled and began to relax. She swung her legs over his head, and landed sprightly on her feet. Smoothing down the hem of her blouse, which had crawled up to just below the lacy edge of her bra, she told him a little about the work she was doing.

"You know that Frank MacPherson's my lawyer, don't you?" He nodded, and she continued as she moved around the big, beautiful room that evoked only an inexplicable loneliness inside her. "I do research, even help write briefs," she laughed softly, "and get into some rip-roaring arguments with one of the other clerks."

Nick nodded, his gaze occupied with the papers in his hands. "And that's all you do, Toni?"

Toni blinked. "Isn't that enough?" she countered with a nervous laugh.

"I would think so," he agreed dryly, his lips tightening unpleasantly, his gaze swinging from her face to the papers grasped in his large hand.

Toni saw him move the top sheet aside and stare down at a picture of her and Dan Ramsey. She moved to his side and looked down forcing herself for a moment to see the picture as Nick would see it.

"Oh no," she groaned. It showed her and Dan Ramsey at lunch, and even she had to admit that they could be seen as less than innocent. They were sitting side by side in a plush banquette, with Toni smiling at Dan as she speared a shrimp from his dish.

"I can explain, Nick," she said, hand reaching to touch the picture. Nick wrenched it away. "He's a junior partner at the law office and he took me to lunch to explain the job. And that's it. He's sort of my boss, Nick, nothing more."

"Your boss," Nick mused, a hint of sadness underlying his sardonic tone. "I wish I could believe that's all he is, Toni." His voice was full of doubt, she thought. He left his perch abruptly and turned to go back to his study.

Jaw tightened, hands clenched into fists at her sides, Toni stared after him. Her hunch was right on target. Nancy Kincaid had to be behind this smear campaign. Never had she felt so frustrated, so totally defeated. She'd thought love was supposed to feel good! Her lips pursed to keep from spitting those very words like bullets at Nick's receding back.

"Go upstairs and change for lunch," Nick ordered over his shoulder as he stepped into his study.

Toni bristled. "Yes, *daddy*," she returned sarcastically.

"What did you call me?" came through clenched teeth as Nick turned around to face her.

Toni smiled woefully. "Isn't it odd, Nick, how alike you and my mother really are? You both forget I'm a *woman*."

"Maybe if you acted like one once in a while," he mocked, and started toward her with a gleam in his eyes. "So you don't think I treat you like a woman?" he said softly, still moving toward her.

"Right," she said, deliberately cold. "You remember I'm a woman only when you get an urge and there's no other female handy."

He stopped advancing. She saw, and relished, that the gleam of desire fizzled out of his eyes. His expression was inscrutable, and for a moment he said nothing. He regarded her coolly, but what thoughts were running through his mind it would have been impossible to guess. Thinking he meant to allow her that one remark without rebuttal, Toni turned and started toward the stairs, but stopped dead when he said: "God in heaven, how could I have fooled myself into thinking you were a sweet, old-fashioned sort of girl?"

Toni looked at him coldly, a wry smile tugging at the corners of her mouth. "It was easy for you, Nick," she said with cutting sweetness. "You're so good at jumping to conclusions." And then she raced up the stairs, away from the murderous glint in his eyes, half fearing and half hoping he would follow. She longed to taunt him until, out of sheer frustration, he would take her in his arms and attempt to master her with his brute strength. But he left her alone, and Toni was strangely desolate.

The following days were sheer hell for Toni. During the daylight hours when Nick was either in his office or at his apartment in the city, she was busy with her own activities. It was the nights that tormented her. Nick seemed almost obsessed with work, bringing a bulging briefcase home with him every evening. He kept himself locked away in his study till the small hours of the morning. He usually had a dinner tray sent into him, which left Toni alone in the big dining room. And then alone again when she went to bed, because Nick made certain that he outwaited her.

Only for odd moments were they alone together, and then Nick made it a point to keep the length of a room between them, speaking only of noncontroversial things when he bothered to speak to her at all. Toni adopted an uncaring mien, but she went around looking like a zombie for all the sleepless hours she spent waiting for him to come to her.

Toni did not know just how long she could survive under the tension that had her in its grip. She made up her mind to have a serious talk with Nick to clear the air at the first opportunity that presented itself.

Such a chance came sooner than she expected. It was Wednesday, her day off, and because Nick always stayed in the city on her days off, Toni had decided to treat herself to a quick breakfast and then a few hours of window-shopping. She was on her way out to her car when Nick drove up.

A deeply warm and expectant feeling settled in her stomach when he left his car and came toward her. She stood very still, hardly daring to breathe as he came to a stop in front of her.

"Come with me." His hand snaked out and curled around her wrist, pulling her roughly toward him.

Toni's heart jumped with joy. At last they were going to talk . . . or *something!* She breathed a sigh of relief, feeling the weight of tension drop from her shoulders. Now was the time to take a chance, to make a clean breast of things, to share the secret she had guarded from him for so long. She would tell him that she loved him and——

But Nick did not take her to the house. He stopped abruptly beside his own car, and she collided squarely into him. He glanced briefly at her, then reached out and opened the door of his car to show her two very hairy, very noisy, and very demanding pups. Toni stared down at them a moment, then started to touch them, a smile of delight slowly curving her lips. But she stopped.

"Pure-blood Irish setters," Nick announced near her ear, making her shiver with desire in spite of her new resolve not to allow him to arouse her. She stepped away from him, fervently thankful that she had not made a complete fool of herself by voicing her earlier thoughts.

Nick stood watching her with a half-doubtful, half-hopeful expression on his face, while Toni gazed at the pups without making a move to touch them.

"Well?"

Toni remained stubbornly mute.

"Don't you like them?" His deflated tone showed her that something had died within him, perhaps a hope he was nurturing that his gift would somehow bridge the gap growing between them.

Toni shrugged. "They're all right," she said coolly, and turned to go.

A hurt look flitted across his eyes, but was swiftly replaced by a wintry expression. "You'll learn to love 'em," he stated with cold assurance. "They'll be your constant companions from now on." He spun around and almost ran across the courtyard and into the house.

Toni sighed in defeat. "Well, that's that," she muttered, her eyes going down to the pups playfully snapping at each other. "Come on. I guess we had better stick together. It looks like Nick's going to ignore you just as he does me." Gathering the two rambunctious pups in her arms, she closed the door of the Maserati and went into the house.

Nick was in the study. She could hear him moving around in there. Lately he seemed to do a lot of pacing, Toni thought and charged it to business worries. Gathering her courage, she walked determinedly toward his door. Business worries or not, he was going to give her some time right now! She raised a hand to knock when the door opened and Nick stood in the doorway. Briefly, he showed surprise at finding her there, then curtly informed her that her mother was on the phone. Toni mentally cursed Catherine's timing.

"Tell her not to use this number again," Nick rasped, stepping aside to let her by.

"*I* didn't give out your number, Nick," Toni gritted through clenched teeth, pushing the pups into his arms. Maybe Nancy did, she thought venomously, hurrying to the hall extension desk. There was no doubt in her mind that Nancy had his private number. And who knew how many other women had it? That thought made her jealous heart jerk and put a serrated edge on her voice.

"Hello, mother."

"Lord, darling, is that how one greets one's mother after a long separation?" Catherine's voice was tinged with amusement. "What's the matter? You and that awful man you married have a tiff?" she teased, and the thought seemed to delight her because she laughed.

Toni clenched her teeth until her jaw ached. "No, mother. He's never home, so how can we fight?" she said unthinkingly.

"So that's how it is," mused Catherine, and Toni ached to be able to call back her thoughtless remark.

"When did you get back, mother?"

"Yesterday, and I told Guido that the first thing I wanted to do was come to San Francisco to see you. Can we have lunch?"

"When?"

"Today?"

Toni glanced through the study door. The room was empty. "Where shall I meet you, mother?"

Catherine suggested the restaurant in her hotel, and Toni readily agreed. She should tell Nick where she was going, she thought, slowly cradling the phone. In the event he was going back to the city, she would offer to stay and have dinner with him. It would be a perfect opportunity for them to talk, to air out their differences.

Toni looked in Nick's bedroom and was about to check the rest of the house when she glanced out the window: the Maserati was gone.

Turning decisively on her heel, she hurried down the hall to her room. She changed into a black skirt and white silk blouse. Around her waist she cinched a wide black belt with silver buckle. She combed her hair away from her face and secured it behind her ears with tiny black combs. Climbing into a pair of black kid ankle-high boots, she draped her purse over her shoulder and left the house.

Driving into the city, Toni convinced herself that the less said about her marriage, the better off she would be. Unconsciously her eyes went up to the rearview mirror, and she noted gratefully that she did not appear at all as unhappy as she felt. Looking back at her was a poised, sophisticated woman of wholesome beauty. She smiled at her reflection. No one would ever guess that beneath her radiant smile she was frightened, and lonely, and that, more than anything, she wanted to be held in her husband's arms and cherished.

Resolutely, she pushed aside her feelings of inadequacy and thrust her chin out defiantly. She would enjoy her time with her mother and not give her problems with Nick another thought.

It was almost one when she parked her car and went into the hotel where Catherine was staying. She approached the reservations clerk and asked for the deAngelis' room number.

"I'm here, darling, right behind you!" cried Catherine effusively, rushing forward to embrace her. "Oh, baby, baby, baby!" She planted a kiss on Toni's cheek, then held her at arm's length to look at her.

"You've changed." Her tone was incredulous, matching exactly the gleam in the eyes that skimmed over Toni's lovely outfit. "You're even more beautiful..." Her voice trailed off wonderingly as she ran her eyes once more over Toni's slender form. "Marriage and the Caldwell millions seem to agree with you," she laughed forcefully.

She *would* include the Caldwell wealth, Toni thought sarcastically. She smiled thinly. *"Nick* is good for me."

"Yes, well, I suppose so," Catherine conceded reluctantly, wrinkling her nose, a habit she had when she was annoyed. "Come along, I'm simply famished."

Famished. Toni frowned, immediately sensing that all was not right with her mother. She followed Catherine slowly into the restaurant, wondering what could be wrong. She sat opposite her at a table near the window facing the street, her concern increasing when she heard Catherine ordering a lunch suitable to bloat even a hungry male. Smiling up at the waiter, Toni ordered a shrimp salad and a glass of wine.

"Wine?" echoed Catherine. "I didn't know you drank in the afternoon."

Toni's lips curled with amusement. "Wine," she repeated firmly, and laughed.

Catherine simpered, "Well, I guess if you're old enough to—" She lifted her eyebrows in a gesture that left no doubt in Toni's mind about what she had meant to say. Toni turned pink with embarrassment.

Oh, if she only knew!

"I'm twenty-five, mother, old enough for a lot of things," she gritted through her teeth.

"Of course you are, darling, of course you are." Catherine placed a condescending hand over hers, but Toni hastily drew her own away. Neither spoke until their drinks arrived.

"Tell me all, darling," urged Catherine with forced eagerness.

"All about what?" Toni asked innocently. She looked at Catherine over the rim of her glass as Catherine lifted a well-manicured hand to her lovely coiffure. A slow smile curved Toni's lips, but she quickly hid it by taking a sip of her wine.

"How are things with you and Nick?"

"Fine."

"He's working hard, I take it from what you said on the phone."

Toni shrugged. "He has a lot to do. I knew that when I married him, I've no complaints."

"I don't believe that, not for a single minute, darling," Catherine contradicted, laughing softly. "It can't be all roses being married to Nicholas," she added in a tone that implied she knew exactly what it was like living with Nick.

"And how are you and Guido?" Toni asked deliberately, wanting only to distract her from the subject of Nick. She smiled encouragingly.

A shadow fell over Catherine's face. "Things could be better," she murmured despondently.

Toni frowned. She knew why Catherine might be having problems with Guido. Nick had hinted that the old man kept her on a very tight budget. Catherine was impossible, of course, and Toni knew she'd hardly been the best of mothers, but the sight of her suffering still pulled at Toni's heartstrings. She couldn't help it. Catherine was her mother and she loved her, despite ample evidence that she didn't always keep her daughter's best interests in mind.

"How so, mother?" she asked softly.

Catherine averted her eyes. "If only—oh, Toni, what difference does it make? You can't help me." She sniffed, then mumbled something Toni did not understand.

"It's money, dear," Catherine admitted. "If Guido

could clinch a deal with the Caldwell Shipping Lines, we would be set for life."

Toni made an annoyed movement and averted her eyes. "Toni, don't turn away from me!" Catherine ordered harshly. Then she was plaintive. "Help me, Toni, please...."

Toni hated to see that pleading look in Catherine's eyes. It made her want to cradle her mother in her arms, as if she were a small child. She drew a deep breath. "How, Catherine?" she asked wearily.

The worried expression lifted from Catherine's face and was immediately replaced by a bright gleam in her eyes. "Oh, little love, you could be a tremendous help to us all!" It seemed to Toni that her mother's eyes glittered maliciously.

"Who is 'us,' Catherine?" Toni queried suspiciously.

Catherine frowned, something she never did—it caused wrinkles, she said. "What difference does it make, Antoinette!"

Antoinette.

Toni smiled grimly and lifted her chin a fraction. "It means the difference between my helping you and my leaving you out on the proverbial limb!" she snapped.

Catherine's next words confirmed her suspicions. "You've always been a very obstinate girl, Antoinette. But, all right! I'll tell you." She paused, and studied Toni's impassive expression. "Will you help me if I tell you?"

"I'll think about it," Toni replied honestly.

"Oh, all right." Catherine seemed to sag. "Adkins and Vincent, two Caldwell vice presidents, are all for selling the line. They think Caldwell has stretched itself too thin." Encouraged by Toni's wry smile, Catherine went on to say that Nick, as chairman of the board, would be able to block the sale, so they were working furiously to prevent him from being elected. She would not say exactly what they were planning, but Toni assumed that they would work stealthily and unscrupulously to steal from Nick not only the shipping line—his pet—but also the entire corporation. And Catherine would be right there with them, up to her smooth elbows in dirty politics.

"What is it you want me to do?" Toni asked, keeping her anger in check only with great difficulty.

"Spy on Nick," Catherine answered swiftly, brightly. "Find out what he's doing and report back to me. I know that he takes work home, pet. Get to it and tell me what he's done so far."

The shrimp salad that Toni had been looking forward to tasted like sawdust in her mouth, but she swallowed it hastily and picked up her wine glass. It was empty. With trembling hands, she clutched her water goblet and quickly drained it.

"You want me to spy on my own husband?" Toni was incredulous. Catherine had gone too far this time, and Toni felt an unfamiliar rage surging in her chest. She remained silent, afraid that if she unleashed her feelings now there would be a terrible scene.

"Oh, would you quit looking at me like that, Antoinette!" Catherine actually squirmed in her chair as Toni leveled an angry glare at her. Again, *Antoinette*. Catherine was getting angry. Toni smiled grimly. The only time her mother became angry and called her Antoinette was when she felt herself cornered. She would then use every dirty trick in the book to cloud the issue, and eventually she would get her own way. *But not this time!*

Toni slid her gaze to her empty wine glass, wondering if she should order another drink.

Catherine's muffled gasp and her muttered, "Oh, no, she's going to ruin everything!" brought Toni's attention sharply away from her thirst.

"What's wrong, mother?" she asked worriedly, noting the stricken look on Catherine's face. When her mother did not answer immediately, Toni twisted around in her seat to follow the line of her gaze. Her stomach lurched sickeningly. Standing in plain view just outside the window was Nick talking to Nancy Kincaid. Toni took a deep, deep breath to quiet her jealous heart, and forced herself to turn away.

Fumbling in her bag, she found a ten-dollar bill and tossed it on the table. "I'm late, mother," she mumbled past the lump in her throat.

"You certainly are, darling," murmured Catherine as Toni hurried away.

Toni's eyes glinted with murderous rage as she brazened her way to where Nick stood with Nancy Kincaid clinging possessively to his arm.

"Nick, darling, how nice of you to come meet me!" she cried, moving closer to her astonished husband. "I hope I did not keep you waiting?" she added as she hooked her arm through his.

The leashed-in fury in his features as he looked down at her sent shivers of fear racing up Toni's spine while the narrowing of his green eyes killed any hope she might have had that he would not embarrass her in front of Nancy.

"You have lousy timing," Nick hissed ominously for her ears alone, and Toni quipped, "I thought my timing perfect!"

Nancy flashed Nick a very provocative smile, and purred, "If you'd only warned me that your wife was going to join us, Nicky, I'd have made reservations for three instead of just us two." Her smile was positively feline.

Grimly, Toni forced a smile to her face and met Nancy's venomous glare with forced calm. Nancy perceptibly tightened her hold on Nick's arm, silently daring Toni to do something about the situation.

Fighting an urge to kick Nick for being so damned blind where Nancy was concerned, Toni started to withdraw, only to be halted by Nick's comment.

"My wife," he said tightly, "was not invited."

Toni's eyes went swiftly to Nancy's face and she noted that the older woman had rearranged her features into a flashing smile that could only be construed as triumphant.

"Of course I wasn't," Toni agreed sweetly, "I wouldn't dream of intruding into any of my husband's ...er...business affairs, Mrs. Kincaid," flashing her a wicked smile.

A cynical hardness crept into Nick's darkly fringed eyes, and Toni guessed he had not liked what she was implying, but she was past caring. She held his gaze unflinchingly, silently daring him to deny what her eyes were seeing.

With a muttered curse, Nick excused himself from Nancy and, taking Toni firmly by the arm, led her around the corner of the building, away from the bemused dark-haired beauty.

"Look, Toni, you don't understand," he began in a quiet, half-pleading tone. "This is—"

"What is there *not* to understand, Nick?" she interrupted with pseudo-innocence. "Your dealings with Nancy are strictly business, aren't they?"

They stared at each other, the air between them crackling with high-voltage tension. Finally, Nick's features softened. Wordlessly, he grasped both her shoulders, saying, "I'll see you at home, Toni," a mixture of command and entreaty in his voice.

"If Nancy lets you go home," Toni taunted, then turned to put a much-needed distance between them.

She struck off aimlessly, her back ramrod stiff, her desire to get away from him eloquently expressed by her hurried steps. Nick quickly went after her, his steps firm and determined.

"Toni!" he called out in an amused voice.

Toni stopped, but did not turn around. She did not want to see the smile that she had heard in his voice.

And then he was standing directly behind her, and his hands were taking gentle possession of her arms. He held her to him for a moment and then, very slowly, he turned her around, wrapping her loosely in his arms.

"If I didn't know better, Toni, I would think you were acting very much like a jealous wife." He smiled down at her, but Toni refused to answer his smile. She sniffed instead. "Toni, if I *asked* you to, would you go home now and wait for me there?"

"No."

"I didn't think so," Nick replied dryly.

"If that's all, Nick . . ." She twisted and squirmed in his embrace, but his only response was the tightening of his muscular arms.

"No. No, it isn't, Toni," he said finally. With that he bent his frame and then brutally covered her mouth with his. Even as angry as she had been, it took only a moment for him to make her respond to his kiss.

"*Now* it is," he said, smiling with satisfaction.

Toni stared after him as he went back to Nancy. How dare he! she fumed. How dare he kiss her, and then blithely walk away to take his mistress to lunch! But she knew that her anger was rooted in jealousy and partially directed at herself, because his kiss left her with a maddening hunger deep in her body.

minutes after ten, looking windblown and drowsy, and in no mood for a confrontation. Her hair curled in wisps over her brow, the play of light on her smooth, golden skin, the languorous gleam in her large grey green eyes...all these were taken in by the man who, tall, assured, and with a sort of sensuous grace in his movements, came slowly toward her, a tentative smile playing about his mouth.

A sudden rush of desire swept through her, and unconsciously Toni stiffened. Nick stopped directly beneath the skylight in the entrance hall, the moonlight slipping through the opaque glass and playing about his handsome features, putting a gleam in his eyes that made them shine like precious stones. Toni moved back a step. She was in no state to fight off the feelings this man could arouse in her. She was, she told herself with an inward sigh, much too...susceptible to his charms. Some inner force, or perhaps his own strong male magnetism, compelled her forward when all she wanted to do was to turn and run. He met her halfway and held out his arms.

"You took your time getting here," he murmured, but there was no censure in his tone. "But I'm happy you're finally here." He took the trembling hand that reached out to him, and very gently pulled her into his warm embrace. "I thought you'd never come home," he whispered, lightly brushing her lips with his. Like feathers, the tips of his fingers fleetingly caressed the skin beneath her jaw, that very sensitive area behind her ear, moving around to tangle in her hair at the back of her neck. A welcome warmth stole over her as Nick's mouth settled with maddening slowness over hers; a delicious sensuality that was as strange as it was pleasant made her tingle to the tips of her toes.

A sigh of contentment slipped between their merging mouths, and at that moment, Toni could not tell from whom it came. Nor did it matter.

The warmth of his breath tickled her nose as he traced the outline of her quivering lips with his tongue.

"Tell me what you're thinking, Toni." Lifting his head slightly, he looked into her eyes, his own darkened with passion. "I had thought to be able to read you like a book, honey, but right now I must confess I cannot honestly tell what it is I see in your eyes. Tell me what's running through your mind this very minute. I need to know," he commanded brusquely, lightly biting her lower lip.

Drawing a quick breath, Toni shook her head. Lord, at this moment she did not even *want* to think, and she shyly admitted as much, lifting herself up to kiss his lips.

Music from his stereo had been floating softly through the air, but Toni had not heard it until Nick drew her farther into the shadows with him.

"Then don't think of anything, Toni," he encouraged her in a voice vibrating with emotion. "Just feel, darling, *feel*." His arms tightening their tender hold on her drew her closer to him and then they were dancing, much to Toni's surprise.

Dazedly she followed his lead, not understanding what had prompted this sweet and loving attitude, but praying that it would last. Between kisses, when he allowed her a moment to draw a breath, to think, Toni told herself she would be content if this loving mood lasted only this one night, but she fervently wished it would last forever.

Their lips touching, their feet moving to the music almost of their own accord, Toni felt Nick's arms drop from around her, and she immediately missed their warmth. Lord, he couldn't be thinking of not finishing what he'd started!

Nick had removed his shirt. As he flung it behind him, he made Toni falter, and she sent her arms around him instantly to keep her balance. Her hands came up against the rippling muscles of his back and for a moment she froze.

"No, honey," he whispered against her mouth. "Don't pull away from me. Don't be afraid to touch me." Laughing huskily, he lifted his head and looked steadily into her eyes. "We have to start somewhere, you and I, love, so we might as well start right here and now."

Her eyes opened wide, they skimmed upward, and met the warm, loving gaze in his. Toni stopped dancing, her nerve ends tingling with expectation, her heart beating wildly against her breast.

"Start what, Nick?" she managed in a low whisper, fighting the shivering sensations that were taking command of her body as his hands moved up and down her back. It was all she could do to keep from begging him to make love to her right then and there.

His large hands came around to cup her face between them. "What do you think, Toni?" His low seductive whisper fanned the flames of her desire until Toni thought she would die from the sweet pain of wanting him. Very slowly he tilted her head back, his marauding fingers tangling themselves in her hair to keep her face beneath his. His dark head moved closer, until she could feel the warmth of his breath like a sweet caress on her cheek.

"That's right, darling," Nick murmured encouragingly when Toni's fingers came up to entwine themselves in the curly black hair that sprouted from the middle of his broad chest. Lightly, tentatively, his lips touched hers, and held, waiting for her to respond. Confused by what she thought was hesitation on his part, Toni unwittingly sent her tongue out to moisten her lips. Nick groaned, and then the kiss that had begun with such aching slowness became almost harshly demanding as he crushed her against his powerful body. Under the practiced mastery of his mouth she felt dizzy with desire; and when Nick's fingers worked the buttons of her blouse, Toni made no effort to resist.

"Toni." His whisper feathered her bangs. His lips traveled across her brow as he maneuvered her out of her blouse. Like branding irons, hot, marking possession, his fingers caressed and kneaded her pliable skin, sending shivers trailing each other up and down her spine. With a low moan rising from her throat, Toni swayed toward her husband.

Nick's lips closed over hers, probing, exploring the sweet recesses of her mouth. Startling sensations ignited themselves in unawakened regions of her body. Toni clung to him, her own fingers twisting into his hair, finding the scalp beneath it and moving sensually against it.

She felt her skirt dropping down around her ankles. She felt him smiling against her mouth even as his fingers were working her free of her bra. Toni found herself blushing, and gratefully hid her face against his chest.

Nick laughed huskily. "Going shy on me, babe?"

Toni's shake of her head silently denied his gentle accusation, but she could not speak. She could not even think. She could only feel, shiver, with his hand moving over one breast in a teasing manner.

His head bent low, his lips found the hollow between her breasts. Toni's nostrils were suddenly assailed by the smell of newly washed hair. Responding to an urge that rose from her inner depths, she bent her head and tentatively pressed her lips to his hair.

Stealing a quick kiss from her parted lips, Nick bent and swiftly scooped her into his arms. Toni smiled dreamily. Her eyes roved over his handsome features lovingly. Whatever else happened, tonight he was hers. Her smile widening, she lifted a hand to brush back a recalcitrant black curl that had fallen across his brow.

"What are you thinking now, Toni?" Nick whispered as he moved toward the gold-carpeted steps to the bedrooms on the third level.

Despite the surge of emotion that held her in its thrall, Toni was afraid to declare her love. She whispered something inane about not wanting to think, and Nick seemed satisfied.

"And you, Nick?" She held her breath, hoping he would say that he loved her.

"I want you, Toni," he replied unhesitantly. He kissed her hard, making her aware of the truth in his words. "I need you, badly," he murmured, nuzzling the sensitive spot behind her ear, nibbling on her lobe. "I want ours to be a real marriage, honey. I want you to be my full-time wife." Toni shivered with delight. She pressed her mouth against his, wantonly seeking the feel of his tongue. Nick stood very still for a moment on the bottom step, savoring her kiss, seeming to delight in her uninhibited response.

This was heaven, Toni thought. Nick's kiss deepened, and at the same time he started moving up to his bedroom again. She quietly struggled to remove her boots, and she heard one and then the other drop just before Nick reached his door. With infinite tenderness he lowered her onto the bed, and gently took off the rest of her clothing. He quickly removed his own, and slipped in beside her. Suddenly she was afraid. Nick already had enormous power over her. What would happen if she made love with him now, only to be abandoned yet again tomorrow? Toni knew it would destroy her.

Nick cradled her in his arms, his mouth settling possessively over her lips, his tongue pushing against her pursed lips for entrance into her mouth.

"No, Nick!" she cried.

"Yes, Toni," he countered. "Oh, darling, it's so right!" His voice, thick with emotion, drowned her protest.

Stubbornly, Toni clung desperately to her resolve not to let him make love to her. Over the pounding of blood in her head, she heard her voice, half-heartedly pleading, "Let me go, Nick, please!"

"Calm down. You're just frightened, love, and there's no need to be," he whispered, kissing her tenderly. "I'll be gentle, love, I promise."

Toni did not want his assurances; she wanted him to go away and leave her alone before she broke down and begged him to love her.

Laughing deep in his throat, he gingerly brought his arms around her, drawing her gently but firmly against his naked body.

"Nick, you promised!" she cried wildly, pushing frantically at his chest, but it was like a solid brick wall and as immovable.

"And what did I promise you, love?" he taunted sweetly against the upright nipple of one tingling breast. Lifting himself up, he pressed his mouth hard against hers. What started as a hard kiss suddenly melted into something wild and wonderful.

"I want you, Toni. God, I've never wanted anyone more!" His hot, heavy breath fanned her cheek as his mouth moved across it, pressing tiny, fiery kisses along the stiff line of her jaw. "I'm on fire, baby, please don't turn me away." His mouth was warm, moist, as it moved over her chin, down the smooth column of her neck, settling almost cruelly upon the pulse beating furiously at the base of her throat.

Toni moaned as urgent hands moved restlessly over her body while Nick's mouth found hers with tender insistence, parting her lips, stealing in to sear her tongue with his. His hands were too experienced; they seemed to know what areas of her body were the most sensitive. A weakness, a lazy, sensuous feeling washed over her, banishing all her desire to push him away. With a sound between a laugh and a sob, she wound her arms around his strong neck and drew Nick's face down, her lips hungrily reaching again for his.

A throaty, sweetly triumphant laugh escaped Nick's lips. He lifted his face from hers. "Still want me to leave you, baby?" he teased, his passion-darkened eyes telling her he would not leave even if she begged him to.

"Oh, no, Nick, please!" She clung desperately to his neck.

His hold on her tightened almost painfully. "I wasn't planning to, love," he murmured breathlessly. His hand moved across her flat belly to unexplored regions. His tongue erotically traced a path around the nipple before his mouth settled over her breast.

"You're mine, Toni, do you hear me?" he whispered fiercely, moving over her.

She *was* his. She wanted to belong to him. And for

tonight at least, Nick was all hers. Tears filled her eyes, and for once they were tears of joy. She had never felt this way, she thought, not even with Bob—especially not with Bob.

But all thought fled as Nick began to move against her, awakening sensations at once excruciating and blissful. Their lovemaking was no longer gentle, and Toni felt a driving passion surge in her limbs again and again until it built to a crescendo of pleasure so intense she thought she would die.

As Toni cried out in ecstasy, Nick whispered hoarsely, "You're mine, Toni, you're mine," and she sensed a note of relief in his voice.

Was there ever any doubt? thought Toni as she clung to him, still trembling, until she fell exhausted into a dreamless sleep.

Even before she opened her eyes, Toni knew that Nick was no longer beside her. A tentative hand went out to touch the spot where his head had rested. The pillow was cold, and she knew instinctively that Nick had already left the house. Her gaze moved lingeringly over the part of the bed that he had occupied.

Her cheeks flushed hotly as she recalled her wanton behavior the night before. She sighed. Strangely, she now felt ill at ease again.

Nick had wanted only one thing from her, and he had taken it. He had made no pretensions. "I want you," he had said. "I need you." He had never once claimed to love her and she, wisely, had kept her love a secret that would remain locked in her heart until he came to her and admitted that he loved her—though when that would be, she could not even guess.

Where was he now, and what was he doing? The thought that he might have gone to Nancy made her violently ill with jealousy. If only he had told her he loved her, she might not feel so wretched now.

It was useless to lie there feeling sorry for herself. Slipping off the bed, she quickly returned to her room and pulled out a robe from her closet. Donning it, she went down to the kitchen to brew a pot of coffee.

Mug in hand, she went out into the terrace. Light crept into the sky as night gently gave way to the new day and the sleeping city across the bay began to wake. Lifting her bare feet to the railing, Toni leaned back in her chair, enjoying the warmth of her coffee and the sight before her eyes. She seemed to be in another world, so high up in the hills, surrounded and sheltered by tall trees. The quiet beauty of the morning evoked a sense of well-being in her.

She breathed in deeply the dew-scented air and was suddenly assailed by fresh doubts. Her eyes went to the lilliputian buildings she saw across the bay and she wondered if Nick was indeed so wrapped up with business, or if he was spending a lot of his time with Nancy. A furious negative shake of her head almost banished her jealous thoughts. She should not be so damned suspicious, she told herself firmly. Surely, after...well, he must feel *something* for her? But, no, she must not put too much emphasis on what had passed between them, nor on those sweet endearments whispered into her ear by a man so obviously adept at seduction. A man did not necessarily have to be in love with a woman to make love to her.

Her heart cried out against that painful truth, and she could no longer stay there looking at the beauty of the morning. Stiff-legged from sitting so long on the redwood chair, she left the terrace and went back into the kitchen.

Nick had given the staff a holiday so that they could be alone, she remembered him telling her last night. As she ran water into a small pan to wash her cup and the few dishes Nick had dirtied the night before, she told herself it was a crying shame that he could not have as easily arranged for Nancy's absence from California—or, better yet, from the whole of the United States!

She had just started to dry the dishes when the doorbell rang. Drying her hands, she went to answer it.

A tall, uniformed messenger stood at her door and greeted her cautiously. "Mrs. Nicholas Caldwell?"

Toni nodded.

"All right, Jack!" he called over his shoulder, and in the next moment the front room was overflowing with flowers.

"What's this?" demanded Toni, backing away as the one called Jack strode forward with a small box in his hands. "There's some mistake!"

"No mistake, ma'am. The minute the shop opened, your husband called in an order for all this. . . ." waving a hand through the air, carelessly indicating the flowers whose mixture of fragrances was already giving her a headache.

"And this?" she demanded, glancing down in surprise as the box was placed in her hands.

"Don't know, ma'am," Jack replied. "A messenger brought it to the shop and said your husband wanted it included with the flowers." He walked away, and followed the other man out of the house before Toni could question him further. She heard them laughing, then the roar of an engine, and then nothing.

Slowly, she opened the box in her hands: a yellow rose, just beginning to open, and beside it . . . a tiny music box that played "Because You're Mine." A short note taped to the side of the box read:

> How I wish I could have been with you this morning, Toni.

Toni held the note to her breast. Smiling dreamily, she wound the music box. She spent the day dreaming.

Toward evening, her spirits still soaring, Toni started out for a walk with the two setters. It was amazing how quickly the pups had grown to look like full-grown dogs, Toni thought as she pulled them to the side to allow a car—Nick's car—to go by. Wagging their tails and prancing around her, they circled round and round until they had her twisted up in their leashes. Toni sat down on the road to untangle herself, and that's where Nick found her a few minutes later.

"Now, there's a pretty sight, indeed," he teased. "Here I am on my way home from a hard day's work, and what do I see but the prestigious Mrs. Nicholas Caldwell III, sitting on the side of the road, tangled up with the dogs. My, my, my!" he teased. "If you cannot cope with two small dogs, honey, how in the world are you going to deal with the houseful of kids I plan for you to give me?" Hunkering down beside her, he soon had her free, and in his arms.

Blushing hotly, Toni hid her face against his chest, and mumbled, "Thank you for the flowers, and the music box, Nick."

"Do I get nothing but a muffled 'thank you'?" He rose to his feet, lifting her up with him.

Shyly Toni lifted herself on her tiptoes to kiss him. Nick stood perfectly still, neither evading nor encouraging, just waiting for her mouth to move beneath his. Only then did he react. He tightened his arms around her, pulling her hard against him.

"Toni!" His mouth pressed down hard until Toni parted her lips in response, allowing his tongue to explore the moist fleshy inside of her mouth. Her breath caught as their tongues merged, and she moved her head in an effort to free herself from the almost unbearable pressure of his mouth, but Nick tightened his hold on her and went back on his heels, lifting her completely off the ground.

After Nick eased her down to earth—at least physically—he led her to his car. Her giggled protests immediately stopped as he pulled from the backseat first a massive bouquet of multicolored blossoms and then two large white boxes. His eyes met hers over the flowers, and she drew in her breath at the softness she saw in those sea-green depths. Almost in a trance, she walked with him into the house, *their* house.

When she opened the boxes, she was again rendered speechless. For out of the first box she drew a flowing turquoise gown and from the second a soft triangular shawl of grey cut-velvet. Nick's eyes were full of laughter.

"Last one to change into evening clothes is a rotten egg!" he called out as he left her to dash up the stairs to his room. Without stopping to ask any questions, she followed his lead, and a mere twenty minutes later stood with him on their terrace.

She was stunned by the beauty of everything around her—the soft feel of the lovely new clothes Nick had bought her, the stunning view of San Francisco, but most of all by Nick himself, resplendent in a rich, traditional black evening suit. She felt overwhelmed by love and good fortune, and even as he moved to embrace her, she somehow knew that this fairy-tale existence would not last long, let alone forever. Her feelings were soon confirmed.

"Toni," Nick said in a seductively soft voice, "we're going to the Top of the Mark tonight. . . ." His voice started to become a little uncertain, and even the thought of dining with him in that fabulous hotel-top restaurant with its stunning view of the city she loved could not chase fear from her heart.

He must have sensed her body tightening up, for even before she could ask him what was wrong, he spoke again. "Toni, I hope you can forgive me . . . again. After dinner, I have to pack some things. I'm catching a flight tomorrow to Seattle, then back to L.A. I'm sorry." Toni found no comfort in the fact that it was obviously difficult for him to tell her this.

"Take me with you, Nick?" she begged, and found herself being put away from him with the same strength of purpose with which he had lifted her into his arms moments ago. Immediately she missed the warmth of his embrace. "Nick?"

"No, Toni, I'm sorry. I'll have a lot to do, and you would only be a distraction."

A distraction. Toni stepped back, then bent down to adjust the strap of her sandal to hide the blush that burned her face. The hurt little girl inside her grown-up mind cried angrily, See? He lifted her up to the heights, then dropped her without warning. Up and down, up and down—the man played her like a yo-yo, and she kept crawling to him for more.

Making a heroic effort to hide her hurt, Toni straightened herself firmly on her feet. "So I'm to be left to my own devices again? For how long this time, Nick?" She forced a smile.

It was long moments before dawning glittered in Nick's green eyes. He smiled, and tried to take her in his arms, but Toni stepped back.

"What's wrong, Toni?" His hand went out to brush aside the silky strands of hair that had fallen across her brow.

"Nothing, Nick," she replied stiffly, taking another backward step. "It's just that we cannot afford to waste any more time. Why don't you pack for your trip now. I—I've just lost my appetite." Turning sharply on her heels, Toni walked briskly away.

He followed her and turned her brusquely around to face him. There was a derisive gleam in the green eyes that glided over her. "I'm going to be gone longer than I'd hoped, Toni. I have to go to Mexico, too. I hope you don't mind being alone. I gave the entire staff these two weeks off, Toni, and they've all scattered to various parts of the country, and to Canada."

Toni blushed, remembering why he had been so generous with the staff. His eyes, when he turned again to look at her, told her that he, too, was thinking about the night before, and she hated the way they raked over her, in a proprietary and challenging manner. What had happened to her promise to herself not to be aroused by him, Toni wondered, feeling a wave of desire flutter through her.

"I don't want to leave you, Toni," he told her quietly. "Please believe that." Turning, he strode swiftly across the room and went into his study.

"Then don't leave me!" Toni begged, but her whisper was drowned out by the closing of the study door. And suddenly she knew that more than anything in the world she wanted to go with Nick.

Firming her resolve and clenching a fist with which to demand entrance into his inner sanctum, she crossed over to Nick's study. But she did not knock. She heard Nick on the phone and froze. Having no desire to eavesdrop on his conversation, she turned to go.

"Damn it, Nancy, you ask a helluva lot of me, you know?" she heard Nick say harshly. "Well, all right, then, it's a date." Silence. Then, "Toni?" guardedly. Toni cringed, and she heard his firm tone. "No, Toni's not going."

Stung by his words, Toni turned and fled to her room.

What a fool she'd been! she thought miserably as she flung off her clothes. Nick was a womanizer. She had always known that. So why had she tried to deceive herself into thinking that she could change him? Men like Nick *never* changed. Angrily, she went into the bathroom and turned on the faucets full blast in the tub.

She should leave him, let him use Nancy to give him an air of respectability—not that that miserable witch could do it!

"Someday . . ." she said through clenched teeth. Someday, she would leave him.

CHAPTER TEN

TONI WAS AWAKE long before her alarm went off at seven, and in the shower before she heard Nick moving around in his room. She had to forego her usual leisurely bath in order to save time; she did not want Nick getting impatient and coming in to find her in the tub. That kind of opportunity she would never give him again, not after last night.

She flushed with the memory. She had been so sure that he had left the house when she heard a door slamming downstairs that she had not worried about locking the bathroom doors. There she was, soaping her breasts, when Nick came into the room, amusedly offering to do the job for her. Not only had he won out on that score, but he had also dragged her out of the tub and made love to her right there on the bathroom rug.

Toni shivered with remembered pleasure. She turned off the shower, left it, and toweled herself off quickly, briskly, pushing away the memory of Nick's lovemaking.

After dressing in white linen blouse and colorful peasant skirt, she ran a comb through her hair, moistened her lips with clear lip gloss, and left her room. A sense of *déjà vu* washed over her as she collided with Nick in the hall, and she shivered involuntarily.

He greeted her with a laugh and a jovial, "Good morning, love."

His arms went around her in a fierce hug. "We have a good day for flying and . . . whatever, don't we?" The *whatever*, she felt sure, was because he believed her plans for the day were not entirely innocent.

An uncomfortable warmth spread through her lower limbs; at the same time she was enraged by his insinuations. "Let me go, Nick!"

Chuckling, he captured the hand that had been raised to strike him. "What's the matter, Toni, can't take a joke anymore?" he challenged softly, giving the imprisoned hand a little shake and then a kiss.

Toni saw that old roguish gleam in his eyes and fought against smiling. "I married *you*, didn't I?" she retorted with nasty sweetness.

His expression sobered swiftly. "I'm glad you're not forgetting that small detail." His voice was deadly quiet, and she sensed a warning underlying his tone. But he grinned. And before Toni could anticipate him, he bent over her, his mouth zeroing in on hers. He kissed her hard, and lingeringly.

Releasing her, he then took her by the elbow and led her out to his car. He wanted to drive her into the city, and she acquiesced. Mutely, Toni stood, too angry to speak, her toe tapping unconsciously as he unlocked the car door for her. Nick, on the other hand, was whistling happily.

She sat in a state of bemusement listening to her husband carrying on a strictly one-sided conversation while her thoughts, against her conscious efforts, kept returning to her eavesdropped conversation between Nick and Nancy.

"Here we are, love, in front of the MacPherson law offices. I'd drive you all the way into the building, but I think Frank would object to that. Hey, Toni, wake up. I know I am the relaxing sort of conversationalist, but not one who would put his own wife to sleep." He shook her slightly, but Toni did not speak. Instead, she opened the door and started to leave the car.

"You could at least kiss me good-bye, Toni," Nick mocked in a dull, defeated tone.

"Oh!" Toni sagged in her seat. Why did he have to say that? Could he have known that she was toying with the idea of leaving him? In her distress, she did not notice that Nick had left the car and come around to her side.

"Toni, is something wrong? Don't you feel well?" He hunkered down and touched her wrist, her brow, her cheek with the back of his hand, then clasped her hands, looking with helpless concern into her face.

"Nothing's wrong," she mumbled and tried to leave the car, but he stopped her. "Let me go, Nick! I said there's nothing wrong!"

Nick lifted her out of the car as he straightened. "Yes, there is, Toni. And you're going to tell me what, or you're not going anywhere. Now, tell me!" He shook her roughly. "I have a right to know!"

Toni bristled. "You have no rights where I'm concerned, Nick Caldwell!" she snapped furiously. "Now, let me go!"

Nick's eyes flashed angrily. "I wish I had the time to shake the truth from you, Toni, but I don't." He released her, albeit reluctantly. "But don't think I'm finished with you. I *am* eventually going to find out what's put that burr under your saddle, I promise you." His features hardened. "I think you know by now that I always get my way." Grabbing her by the shoulders, he drew her to him and kissed her hard. "I'll see you in a few days, Toni Caldwell," emphasizing the surname with pride.

Toni stared after him. For a moment she wished she didn't have so many business appointments that day. She would have been tempted to go cry on Fannie's shoulder in New Orleans. Instead she walked briskly into the building and slipped into the elevator just as the doors were closing.

By the time she reached her floor, Toni's determination to leave Nick had deepened. But she knew she could never break her share of the bargain without hating herself. If only she could help Nick win the chairmanship, she would feel free to leave. He wouldn't mind then. After all, she reasoned, that was his only motive for marrying her in the first place!

That morning, before her resolve could weaken, Toni took Frank aside and questioned him casually about the coming vote at Caldwell Industries.

"Nick's a bit of a maverick," Frank had commented, "and he's never made much of an effort to soften up the stockholders who could swing the vote in his direction. Many of the most important ones are close neighbors of yours, you know. At any rate, as 'playboy bachelor,' I suppose Nick thought they would snub him, but now . . . who knows?"

Before MacPherson could grow suspicious, Toni changed the subject, asking his advice about a case she was working on.

Later that day, Toni obtained a list of the Caldwell stockholders from the office files and left for home, hoping that she had found an honorable way out.

Three days later Toni woke to the sound of the telephone.

"Good morning, Mrs. Caldwell," greeted the husky voice that had the power to weaken her knees. Toni leaned sleepily against the hall wall, fighting to stay awake. "You'll miss a third of the world's delights if you sleep past six o'clock, didn't you know that?" Nick's masculine laugh tingled through her drowsy body, jerking her fully awake.

Through sleep-hazy eyes she peered at the clock on the wall. "Nick, it's only three in the morning! Where are you?" she demanded suspiciously, wondering if he was in some Mexican bar, drinking his fill of tequila and getting sentimental about his neglected wife in California.

"Flying right above you." He drew a ragged breath, then, "Toni . . . do you suppose we can call a truce for one day and spend it together?"

Her traitorous heart soared! "A truce, Nick," she agreed swiftly, not giving herself a chance to consider telling him no. They needed to talk, and what better time than now?

"See ya!"

The telephone went dead. Toni stared at the silent instrument in her hand, then slowly replaced it on its cradle.

At six o'clock, a roguish Nick Caldwell walked out to the terrace where Toni was having a cup of coffee.

"Jeans, Nick?" Toni's eyes were dazzled by the change in her husband. She ran her gaze over him appraisingly, liking the way his faded jeans fit over his muscular thighs and long legs. His knit shirt stretched tautly across broad shoulders, followed the trim line of his body, and was neatly tucked into the narrow waist of his jeans. She smiled. "Not bad," she approved. "But why, Nick?"

Nick grinned. "I thought if I couldn't beat you, I might as well join you. But you outclass me today—a surprise for my homecoming?" he teased. He toyed with the lace at her throat, then ran his hands down her slender form to the long skirt of patchwork brown and tan velvet that so elegantly complemented the long-sleeved linen blouse she was wearing. Nick lifted his hand to the cameo locket at her throat.

"May I?" He opened the locket, and gazed curiously at the tiny pictures it contained: Jamie MacGregor at nineteen and a sweet-looking Catherine at twenty-one.

Toni could hardly breathe. A wave of now-familiar emotion coursed through her body, making her shiver. The shiver was not missed by those dancing green eyes alert to her every movement. Very gently Nick closed the locket and drew Toni into his arms. He kissed her, tenderly.

"Do we go out, honey, or do we stay here and play house?"

Toni shivered involuntarily. Shaking her head, she tried to pull away.

Nick sighed with genuine regret. "I guess we go out."

"Just give me a moment to change," Toni pleaded. She pushed out of his arms and escaped to her room.

In half an hour, they were breakfasting in the city. Nick would not allow Toni to dawdle, and hurried her through breakfast of toast and coffee, then back to his car. He seemed quite anxious to leave San Francisco, but Toni was too bemused to complain.

"Where are we going?" she asked curiously when Nick left the freeway. Off and on she had dozed while Nick drove north, and now she had no idea where they were.

"To a place called Anchor Bay."

"How quaint," she laughed. "And where is this Anchor Bay?"

Nick laughed. "About sixty miles south of Fort Bragg. Now, do you know any more than you did before?" He chuckled, and reached over a hand to tousle her hair. "It's about a hundred and twenty miles north of San Francisco. It's secluded, near the beach, and..." he paused, flashing her a wicked grin before he continued in a relieved tone, "no one knows where we'll be."

Nick slowed down, then turned onto a dirt road. He drove through a wooded campground completely hidden from the road by towering redwoods and lush vegetation. Toni took note of tents of all sizes, motor homes, vans, small and large pick-up trucks, and even several motorcycles all loaded down with camping equipment. Passing behind the crowded beach, Nick drove the Maserati through the woods along a rutted dirt track, and parked near the edge of a tall bluff. He led Toni down a steep rocky trail, then helped her over a huge boulder projecting toward the sea.

At the last moment, Toni lost her footing on a slippery rock and fell to her knees in the water. Nick laughed uproariously at her startled expression, then pulled her to her feet.

"Ooh, this is lovely, Nick." Toni glanced around with dazed eyes. They were standing at one end of a tiny secluded cove with pristine white sand. Large, slate grey boulders surrounded the cove, sheltering it and concealing it from inquisitive eyes. "You might have warned me to roll up my jeans," Toni derided playfully, glancing at her dripping pants.

"You could always take them off——"

"Forget it!"

"I thought maybe you might like a swim?" Nick suggested, his tone innocent, putting down the wicker picnic basket he had carried from the car.

"I didn't bring a suit," Toni said.

"I don't mind."

Toni laughed nervously. "I'll just bet you don't!" She dropped down onto the blanket he had spread on the sand.

"Coward!" Nick hissed into her ear, and laughed as he wrapped his arms around her waist and tumbled her down on the sand.

He convinced her he would not take advantage of her, and finally Toni agreed to go for a swim with him. They undressed, and then ran quickly into the water. It felt ice cold. Toni shrieked, and Nick was immediately beside her, offering the warmth of his arms.

"No, thanks," she quaked, moving away from him,

her arms folded across her quivering breasts. "That kind of warmth I can do without today, thank you." If she allowed him to make love to her, she knew she would never want to leave him.

Nick's eyebrows went up sardonically, and he shrugged. "All right, honey, but if you should change your mind..."

"I won't," she assured him hastily.

They dove into the depths, and eventually Toni relaxed in the water. Nick began to tease her, pulling her farther down and holding her underwater until she felt her lungs would burst for lack of air; or just trapping her legs so she could not kick to get away from his roaming hands. He would follow her up for air, then push her under and hold her down, kissing her, fondling her, his experienced hands moving over all the most sensitive areas of her body to arouse her to a fever pitch of sensual excitement.

Toni came up, sputtering, gasping for breath. "You know, Nick Caldwell, you're a real pest when you want to be!"

"Well," he countered petulantly, making a face, "you won't let me do anything else!"

"I'll let you feed me," she said, deliberately ignoring the meaning behind his words.

"Come along, then." He swam ahead to the edge of the water.

He would, Toni thought dismally. She treaded water, and wondered how she was going to come out with him watching her. It was evident he was not going to budge an inch from where he sat on a boulder, letting the sun's rays dry him.

"Come on out, Toni Caldwell, I thought you were

hungry?" he teased, stretching back on the boulder, bold and arrogant in his nakedness.

Toni sighed in defeat. She knew what he was doing, and, damn him, it was working!

"All right, Nick," she called out, beginning to swim to him. "You win," she whispered under her breath. He would always win, she decided as she came out of the water, and went into his arms.

Laughing triumphantly, Nick wrapped her in a checked tablecloth he had in his picnic basket, then very gently lowered her down to the blanket.

His warm mouth trailed fire across her cheek and up and down the soft column of her neck. His breath fanned her skin, silkily, a caress as soft as a butterfly's wings. Leisurely, he peeled off the tablecloth, exposing the beauty of her body to his hungry eyes. Dazedly, Toni watched him bend toward her. His mouth came down over hers, maddeningly slow at first, igniting a fire in her veins. Then, as her traitorous body responded to the thrill of his hands, his mouth became masterfully sensuous, even arrogant in its dominion.

"Oh, love, how I missed you." The words preceded a light nibble on her lobe.

"You should've taken me with you," she muttered, and with a lurch of her stomach remembered who had taken her place the last few days. *Nancy*. He had had her to warm his bed the past few nights. Angrily she pushed against the hard wall of his chest, but she could not move him. She cursed him in exasperation.

"Toni, what is it?"

Toni clamped down on her back teeth, and refused to answer him.

Nick's expression went hard with determination. "All

right, Toni, let's get it all out in the open." He lifted himself slightly off her, but not enough for her to scramble out from under.

"I don't intend to put up with any more of this on-again, off-again routine of yours. You wax hot and cold with me, and I don't like it. I'd rather have you hot all the time." He smiled, but the warmth normally found in his eyes when he teased her was missing, and his smile suddenly seemed grotesque on his handsome mouth.

"Look, Toni, I don't know what's going through that suspicious mind of yours, but I did not go from you to some other woman, if that's what you've been thinking."

Nick was resting on one elbow, waiting for her to speak, but not very patiently. She blurted out her accusation. "You took Nancy Kincaid with you to Mexico!"

"Like hell I did!" Propping his hands on either side of her, Nick leaned over her and stared down into her face, his features hardened into a frown that eventually gave way to a quizzical expression. "Who told you I had taken Nancy to Mexico?" There was no anger in his voice, only an edge of curiosity.

"I heard you telling her, on the phone, that you would give her a lift when you were planning your trip." Her voice was so low Nick had to bend down to hear her.

Then, to her surprise, he started laughing, arching his head back so that his Adam's apple bobbed up and down as he gave vent to his mirth. Toni detected a faint hint of relief in his laughter.

"Oh, Toni, you jealous little cat! I gave Nancy a lift, all right, but only to the airport. I went to Mexico, stayed there with my manager and his family, the Guerreras; and Nancy went off to cause mischief to her ex-husband, poor sucker."

She stared up at him, taking in every detail of his face, searching his expression for a sign that would tell her whether or not he was lying to her. He did not seem to be, but then how could she know for sure?

Nick seemed to sense her thoughts because he went to work on her, slowly and sensually, cunningly calling upon past experience and every erotic trick he knew to thaw her resistance. He used his body to keep her from escaping him, while his hands and his mouth played a sensual song over her body.

"Toni . . ." His voice was husky with tenderness, vibrating in soft eroticism against the sensitive spot beneath her ear. Toni shivered.

"Nick, I——"

"Shhh. Don't talk, baby." He kissed her with calculated slowness, until Toni felt like screaming for him to quit tormenting her. "Later . . . much later, we'll talk, I promise."

Toni could no longer help herself. Lifting her hands to his chest and moving them exploringly up and around his neck, she tangled her fingers in the hair at his nape. His breathing quickened, his heart hammered out his need against her breasts. Her own heart beat in tune to his, a wild singing joy coursed through her body in response to the pressing urgency of his hard, muscular thighs.

"Love me, darling, love me," Nick begged hoarsely as he moved over her.

Toni sighed with satisfaction, clinging to him as their bodies merged, moving in response to Nick's husky urgings, compensating with loving willingness for what she lacked in experience. This was what poets and lyricists wrote about, this sharing of a time in space, this joyous blending of two souls. Up, up, up to the peak of the mountain they traveled, then slowly, like a feather floating in the wind, they spiraled downward until, at last, they lay enervated beside each other.

Slowly, she became aware of the sounds of the water lapping to the shore, seagulls flying overhead, echoes of the merrymakers coming from the campground. She felt Nick's arms relaxing around her, heard his breathing becoming more regular.

He nuzzled her hair with his cheek. His warm breath was a soft caress on her ear as he whispered, "Let's never go home, Toni. Let's just stay here forever, making love and just getting to know each other."

Toni nodded, and turned to kiss one masculine nipple. What a wonderful dream, a cove to themselves, without telephones, without Caldwell Industries, but, particularly, without all the Nancy Kincaids who would not stay hidden in her husband's past.

"Wanton," he accused, smiling, and kissed her. He then drifted off to sleep.

"I just want to love you," Nick whispered in his sleep. Beside him, Toni turned to look at him, and wondered if she ought to wake him before he divulged any secrets. But, Lord, how she wanted—*needed*—to know if she was the one who monopolized his dreams. He must have felt her moving beside him, because he opened his eyes, and grinned.

"Insatiable woman! Can't you let a man have his rest?" he teased, sending out his arms to hug her to him.

"It's getting late, Nick," she whispered against his mouth.

"You have an appointment somewhere that I don't know about?"

Toni laughed. "No, silly. It's just that the sun's going down, it's getting cold here, and the tide's coming in."

Lifting himself up on one elbow, Nick looked around them. "Ah," he sighed, but it was not a happy sigh. "You're right. Looks like we're going to have to give up our lovely little hideaway." Shaking his head ruefully, he reached out to gather their clothes.

They dressed in moody silence, somewhat reluctantly. Nick kept looking at her, his expression unreadable. Toni wished she could tell what he was thinking, but he was such a close-mouthed individual, she would not find out even if she dared to ask him. She shrugged, consoling herself with the thought that he had promised they would talk later.

They left Anchor Bay with the sun at their backs. Toni's hopes of getting Nick to discuss their relationship dwindled with every mile, finally dying as they came to the outskirts of San Francisco. Nick was unnervingly quiet, and she was afraid to make him angry by forcing conversation. It struck her that he might be regretting having taken the day off to be with her. Perhaps he regretted letting his guard down with her? Toni looked at his stiff profile, wishing she had the nerve to force a showdown.

They stopped in the city for dinner, and Toni could not remember when she had felt so alone in a crowded room. Nick sat across the table from her, but he seemed to be miles away, moodily staring at something beyond her. He hardly touched his dinner, but he drank heavily. Toni ate hungrily, hoping her example would awaken his appetite.

They arrived home after one in the morning, and Nick seemed suddenly too tired, too drunk to care how he sounded. "I'm going to bed," he growled, preceding her into the house. "I've got a damnable headache."

"I thought it was the woman who was supposed to get the headaches?" Toni teased, stepping into the entry carrying the basket and blanket Nick had left sitting beside the car.

Nick slanted her a quick, frigid glance. "And *I* thought it was the man who—" He stopped, shook his head, then whirled around and almost ran up the stairs to his room.

Toni blinked, totally confused. "Damn you, Nick, you're driving me crazy!" she screamed after him, her patience with him completely exhausted. Her words returned to taunt her in the empty house.

"I must be crazy," she muttered, her tone loaded with self-contempt. If she weren't would she still remain in love with Nick?

The telephone rang, and Nick was immediately in the hall, his hand reaching out for the instrument almost as if he had made an appointment with someone to call him at that hour. Could it be anyone but Nancy? Toni's stomach muscles tightened into knots when she heard the sound of his rich male laughter ringing through the empty house. Marshalling her emotions and stiffening her backbone with the last few shards of pride remaining to her, she went quietly past Nick at the phone and into her room. She knew that a few minutes after he hung up, he would be on his way back to San Francisco, but she was too tired to care. At least, that was what she told herself.

CHAPTER ELEVEN

UPON RETURNING HOME from work the next day, Toni noticed that Nick's Maserati was still gone. As she had predicted, Nick had slammed out of the house right after he had hung up on his "mysterious" caller last night, and he was still away. *On business, no doubt,* Toni thought bitterly, her face contorted with sarcasm.

"Damn!" The word echoed eerily around her. As usual, she found the heavy stillness of the empty house utterly hateful. The dogs, evidently hearing her come in, had started to howl.

Castor and Pollux, as Toni had whimsically named the setters, wagged their tails furiously when Toni went out to their pen. Yapping and running around in excited circles when they saw her, they somehow managed to lift Toni's spirits.

"We're alone again, fellas." After having her face

thoroughly licked in greeting, she attached their leashes to their collars and led them to the front yard. Wondering why Nick had not told her where he was going or how long he would be away, she opened the gate and coaxed the dogs out to the road.

One of her neighbors, a tiny lady with a mass of silvery hair and a toy poodle that matched her hair, was coming out of her house when Toni started down the hill. For a moment Toni's attention was arrested by the silvery toy poodle. Her momentary distraction gave her rambunctious pups time to decide to get playful. They began to strain at their leads to get at the poodle, pulling Toni along with them.

"Oh, no, you don't!" Toni cried firmly. She pulled and pulled, but of course, she was no match for them. They ran away with her easily. Toni clung helplessly to the leashes, her feet barely touching the ground as the dogs took off at a dead run.

Toni was sure she would lose her balance and have a nasty fall when the setters slowed of their own accord. They'd dragged her to within a few feet of the poodle. Now they were sniffing curiously and wagging their tails.

A bit winded and embarrassed but otherwise unharmed, Toni turned to face the elderly lady, who was watching her with benevolent amusement.

"Please forgive me for . . . the sudden intrusion. I'm afraid I lost control for a moment," stammered Toni.

"Don't apologize, dear, I'm just glad you weren't hurt. In fact, I'm delighted to meet you. I am speaking to the lovely new Mrs. Caldwell from up the hill, am I not?" The woman extended her hand with a winning smile. Toni grasped it gratefully, murmuring that she was pleased to meet one of her new neighbors at last.

Idly Toni wondered if she had her hair tinted to match the poodle's or vice versa.

"Well, my name's Jana Cooper, and I live here." She came to a stop in front of a wrought-iron gate that closed off a Spanish-style courtyard. "I and my four friends. Would you like to come in and visit for a while? Perhaps you'd like a cup of tea? You must be a bit shaken up from your...involuntary run."

Toni smiled. She liked this woman immediately. "That would be nice," she said, glancing up the hill to her own house. There was no one waiting for her up there, and—she wished the thought had not entered her mind, but it did—Jana Cooper and the other women who lived at 303 Fircrest Lane were all Caldwell Industries stockholders, and she knew they had objected to Nick's being chairman because of his "excesses." Perhaps if they liked her, they might change their minds about him. Thinking of him reminded her that he had not even bothered to tell her where he was going, and she stiffened her shoulders with resolution. She would do everything she could to encourage these women to help Nick get his chairmanship, and then she would leave him.

Her heart jerked at the thought, but she ignored its painful protest, and accompanied Jana to the house, feeling a little guilty about her secret purpose.

Toni was busy every day, and she was happy. Or rather, she was usually too tired to think how truly unhappy she was.

Nick had returned from his trip a brooding stranger. They were seldom together, and when they were Nick made it a point to remain barely civil.

This is ridiculous, Toni told herself one morning when

she heard Nick going into his study. She had hoped to waylay him in the kitchen when he came down for his morning cup of coffee, and somehow force him to talk to her. Taking a quick sip of her coffee, she pronounced it good enough for Nick. With Mrs. Mansfield visiting a sick sister in Arizona, the chore of making coffee had fallen to her, but Nick was never home to drink it.

"But he's going to drink it today," she promised herself and, grabbing the pot and a cup from the counter, she left the kitchen and walked determinedly toward his study. Drawing a deep breath to calm her racing heart, she walked into his inner sanctum without bothering to knock. Her heart was in her throat as she walked stiffly toward his desk.

"You're a workaholic, Nick Caldwell," she accused in a voice that sounded strange even to her. "I'll bet that I could just disappear and you'd never even know I was gone unless the phone rang out in the entry and you had to get up to answer it yourself!" Without looking at him, afraid she would find an angry or hateful expression on his face, she set his cup down and filled it.

"I'd know, Toni." Nick smiled thinly. "Believe me, I would know." He took a sip of his coffee, looking at her over the rim of his cup.

There was more than arrogance in his tone; Toni sensed a veiled warning in his words. "Oh, you would, would you?" she teased, her voice a bit husky.

"I would, Toni, believe me," he replied stiffly. He studied her in a way that stripped her of her cocky veneer and sent a rivulet of liquid fire through her veins.

Though the coffee was very hot, he drained his cup in one gulp and stood up. "Someday I'll show you how I'd know, but not now. Now I have to go back to the office. Since it's already late, Toni, I think I'll stay at the apartment in town and get an early start on things tomorrow."

"Are you sure you can't make it back in time for dinner?"

The green of Nick's eyes darkened with anger. Dropping the papers he had picked up, he came around the desk.

"Are you asking me for assurance that I'll be gone all night, Toni?" He moved so quickly, Toni was startled and let out a yelp. His hands went out and curled painfully over the fleshy part of her arms, drawing her up and against him. Toni recognized the danger signals in his glittering green eyes, and went limp in his arms.

"The reason I was asking, Nick, is because you evidently forgot that we were invited to dinner at Jana's."

His expression relaxed swiftly with dawning. He smiled guiltily. "Oh, Toni, I did forget. But really, I have to go. Tell them I'll take a rain check, all right?"

Toni's upper arms tingled with renewed feeling when he released her. She glanced down first at her right and then at her left arm, and noted that his thumbs had left their mark. Not to be outdone, his fingers had left their brands on the insides of her arms.

"I'll bet when you were a little boy, you pulled the wings off flies for kicks," she muttered as he passed through the door.

He turned. "Were you talking to me?"

Toni did not deign to reply, and in a moment he was gone.

"Just bring yourself . . . and Nicholas, of course," Jana had told her when she invited her to dinner, but Toni had felt uncomfortable about showing up empty-handed. So, armed with a lemon meringue pie she had bought, she knocked on the Cooper door. She walked in expecting to see only the five women who had recently become her friends. Instead, she walked into a room filled with elderly people, most of whom she did not know. Feeling out of place, she approached Jana and started to offer a lame excuse about why she couldn't actually stay.

Jana would not let her go. "Nonsense! I asked these people here particularly to meet with you and Nicholas. You see, these..." encompassing all her friends with a sweep of her dainty hand, "are all that's left of the original stockholders of Caldwell Industries. All except for Frank McPherson, whom you already know. He couldn't be here tonight."

"Neither could Nick," said Toni apologetically "Business, you know." She was very uncomfortable, and wished she had never come. But it was too late. She was here. Further, Jana had her by the arm and was leading her around the room, introducing her to everyone as "the sweet young woman whom Nicholas married."

Something in the pit of Toni's stomach shriveled into a tight little knot. These were the people she had cold-bloodedly thought to cultivate, to sway over to Nick's side in the miserable battle for control of Caldwell Industries. Looking at the various smiling faces as she was welcomed into their group, she experienced a feeling of self-contempt so heavy it made her feel nauseated. Suddenly she wished she had never set out to make their acquaintance.

Over a dinner of oysters Rockefeller, pressed duck, tossed green salad, and the pie that Toni had brought, the people she knew held Nick's future happiness in their hands quizzed her about herself and her husband. They made no pretense about what they were doing. They wanted to hear from Toni's own lips that Nick had settled down and was now the respectable man they wanted to head *their* corporation. Toni vacillated between being thankful Nick was not there and cursing him in her mind for being absent. She answered truthfully and without embellishment each question they posed, hoping she was helping them see Nick in a favorable light.

"Well, I must say that you're nothing like what we dreaded Nicholas would marry," announced an old gentleman who claimed to have been a childhood friend of her grandfather's. He glanced around the room, apparently seeking approval. The smiles he received from his friends made his grin wider.

Toni experienced a twinge of disappointment. Was that all?

It did indeed seem to be all that was to be said concerning Nick. Toni did not know whether to feel sad or glad that no one had mentioned the struggle for power currently going on at Caldwell.

When at last she left that night, Toni was not certain that she had done Nick any good. She shook away the feeling of inadequacy she was beginning to feel and consoled herself with the thought that at least no one had said anything derogatory about Nick.

Smiling with a strange sense of relief, Toni let herself into the house. She shivered. This was the one thing she would never get used to—walking into an empty house, particularly at night. She hugged herself in an attempt to stop her shivers, which she knew were rooted in nervousness rather than cold. On tiptoes, she went across the entryway, praying that the dogs would not hear her coming in and set up their howling to be let out.

Not that they would waken anyone——

A faint sound coming from the direction of the kitchen interrupted her thoughts, and she froze with fear.

"Wh—who's there?" she quivered. In the dark she could not judge the distance to the front door, but she instinctively knew that she would never reach it before the intruder reacher her, not the way her knees had weakened.

A tall, ominous figure disassociated itself from the dark alcove off the kitchen and began moving slowly toward her.

Nick! How long had he been sitting there in the dark? And why?

Toni's relief was so great, she had started toward him when something about his rigidity stopped her. In a dark suit, with a dark turtleneck beneath the double-breasted coat, he reminded her of an ancient mariner with piracy and ravishment in mind.

"Where have you been?" he demanded finally, in a deadly quiet voice that was menacing in its intensity. Toni shivered involuntarily.

What was the matter with him? He *knew* where she had gone tonight. Toni stared dumbfounded at his advancing form. She gulped in air as he continued toward her, staring helplessly into his diamond-hard look when he came to a stop beneath the skylight. She darted a quick look over her shoulder at the door. It seemed to be miles away! But if she did not move now, something told her she might never move again! Fear gave her wings. But her jerking movements galvanized Nick too, and she was caught before she had taken too many steps toward freedom.

"Now, where in hell have you been? Who with this time?" His arms tightened like vises around her until Toni found herself struggling just to take a shallow breath. She stared into his angry features with a terror mounting almost to paralysis. She was certain Nick could hear the pounding of her heart, but he seemed oblivious to everything but his need to punish her.

"Nick, you're hurting me," she choked out in a tiny, pitiful whisper. "Nick, please let me go!"

A horrible, chilling laugh erupted from Nick's taut mouth. "Maybe you think I don't have the right to know where you go, who you see, what you do, but you're wrong, Toni. Dead wrong!"

Toni hated the sound of his voice at that moment. Out of sheer desperation, she moved closer to him and rested her face against the soft knit of his shirt.

"Oh, God, Nick, I just don't understand what's gotten into you!" she cried, rubbing her cheek against his chest.

Nick slowly relaxed his hold on her, and he held her to him for a moment without speaking. Toni felt his thumping heart return to a normal beat, and again wondered why he was so angry.

"There's nothing you need to understand about me, Toni, except that until *I* decide otherwise, I am your husband in every sense of the word, with certain rights. One of those rights is faithfulness from my wife, 'boughten' or not!"

She stood perfectly still in his arms, thinking back to the night of his crazy proposal. Had he not said that it was up to *her* when she wanted to "slink away"? And then...oh, her heart soared. *Nick was jealous!* Toni smiled, and gently nuzzled her cheek against his arm.

"I was having dinner with Jana and her friends, Nick,"

she told him quietly. "I told you about it, remember?"
She pressed her cheek to his chest, liking the feel of that
strong wall behind which beat the heart she yearned to
win. "You told me you wouldn't be home tonight so I
didn't worry about the time. You finished with your
business early?"

At her question Nick flinched. His arms fell from
around her so fast, she almost fell, and before she could
form the words to ask him what she had done wrong this
time, he turned and walked away.

What was it that had made him turn so abruptly from
her, as though he could no longer bear to touch her? Toni
stood quietly watching him, her grey green eyes shimmering with tears while her mind raced with chaotic
thoughts. *Guilt*. The word lodged itself in her brain.
Guilt. Guilt. Guilt. Nick had been *angry* until she asked
him if he had finished with his business early. Business!
she jeered mentally. More like monkey business! Abruptly,
she turned toward the stairs.

"Where are you going?" he snapped without turning.

Toni stopped with her hand on the bannister. "Up to
my room, Nick." She took the first step.

A heavy sigh escaped him, then he was walking across
the room to her. He reached out both hands, almost
touching her. Toni shivered out of his reach and took
another step up. She heard his sharply indrawn breath,
and turned in time to see a hurt look flitting across his
eyes. His tone, when he spoke, was one of utter weariness.

"Toni, please don't go."

Toni's compassionate heart came into play, urging
her to go to him, to hold him, to comfort him, to assure
him that she loved him. But she stood as though rooted

to the stair, unable to go to him and yet unable to leave.

Nick's eyes roved almost lovingly over her, lingering on her lips. For a moment he stood there, just drinking in the sight of her. Then he moved up the first step and took her hand.

"I'm sorry, Toni. I don't know what happened to me when I came home and found you gone." A slow grin spread his lips. "I guess I finally got a taste of what I've put you through, leaving you here alone all the time, and I didn't like it." The unconscious circular motion of his thumb on her palm had an oddly seductive effect.

"Forgive me, Toni?"

"Only if you tell me exactly what to forgive you for, Nick." Her voice sounded like a frog's croak, and she blushed.

His smile faded, leaving in its wake a shadow that was no more than a derisive grin. "For everything, Toni."

Even Nancy? she questioned in her mind, still caught in the grip of a suspicion that Nick had been with Nancy and was now feeling guilty about it.

"Everything?" she asked doubtfully, quirking a mocking eyebrow. Nick grinned and gave her hand a squeeze.

"Come for a walk with me, Toni." He pulled on her hand and forced her down to him.

Outside, the dogs begged to be released from their confinement, and Toni smiled with grim amusement.

"Should we take them?" she asked, thinking it was Nick's turn to be pulled every which way by his dogs. He seldom, if ever, was around when the silly things were being unmanageable.

Hooking his arm through hers, Nick pulled her toward the front door. "Not this time, Toni. I don't want to share you with anyone tonight. I want to have you all to myself.

I want to see you in the moonlight, pretend that we've just met, and do everything like I should've done it at the beginning." He grinned, and her heart fluttered at the sight of his familiar roguish expression.

"Ah, now," she breathed, hugging his arm to her, "this is the Nick I know from New Orleans."

"And like?"

"I beg your pardon?"

"The saying, babe, is 'this is the so-and-so I know and love' but in my case, I will settle for 'like' and count myself very lucky."

Toni stared. Was he saying what she was hearing? Or, rather, was he hinting at what she had hoped to hear?

Toni remembered Nancy in time, and did not blurt out that she loved him. "The Nick I met in New Orleans, I liked. He seemed...uncomplicated, somehow. A likable fellow, considering his bossiness. The Nick I've been seeing lately..." She shrugged.

"So, will the real Nick Caldwell please bow, is that it?" She nodded, but he did not reply to the plea in her eyes. Toni wondered if he even knew which one he was.

Nick opened the door and urged her outside, putting an arm around her shoulders as they started to walk down the hill.

With his arm across her shoulders, his fingers lightly caressing her arm, Toni's mind drifted away from the unanswered question that lay between them.

CHAPTER TWELVE

MAYBE HE DOESN'T feel he has to *tell* me he loves me, Toni consoled herself with that thought as she glanced at Nick. For the past week they had been so blissfully happy, she did not want to rock the boat by making waves now. Maybe later. . . .

"I wish we could have stayed home," Nick said as he brought his car to a stop in front of Catherine and Guido's showy new house in Big Sur.

"Me too," Toni sighed, nuzzling her cheek against his arm. Glancing up at his face, she found him frowning.

"Something wrong, Nick?"

He grinned. "No, honey. I was just thinking . . . Let's go in, say hello and good-bye in the same breath, and skip out on them."

Skip out on a Christmas party? Particularly one given by her mother? Toni smiled doubtfully. "Oh, Nick, should we? We already agreed to spend the night!"

"Yep. I heartily recommend it. We don't need this group, Toni." He chucked her lightly on the chin. "And your mother will be overjoyed to see me leave, believe me." His smile faded, and Toni saw his jawline tighten.

Toni frowned. She wished Nick and Catherine were on better terms. "All right, Nick, if you think it's all right."

"That's why we shouldn't have come," he mumbled. Then he grinned. "Just stay close to me, honey, and when I say 'go,' we'll sneak out the back door. Believe me, they won't even know we've gone." Reaching into the back seat of his Maserati, he lifted the gifts Toni had bought for Catherine and Guido, then they left the car.

It was as Nick had said. The crowd was so noisy, Nick and Toni's entrance into their midst went unnoticed for several minutes. Toni took the gifts from Nick, found Catherine's tree, and arranged them neatly under it. When she rejoined Nick, he suggested that they look for the back door.

"Too late!" Toni hissed when she saw her mother coming toward them. Nick winced.

"Darling!" Catherine rushed eagerly toward them, holding her arms out to Toni, crushing her in a motherly embrace, while her eyes coldly assessed Nick.

"And how are you, too, Catherine?" Nick mocked sweetly.

"Fine, Nicholas, and you?"

Before Nick could reply, they were interrupted by Nancy Kincaid. Toni smiled. Driving here with Nick, she had promised herself that nothing was going to spoil her evening. She returned Nancy's sardonic glance with a sweetly mocking smile. Nancy frowned, furiously.

"Hello, Nicky." Like a feline anticipating wetting her whiskers in a bowl of warm cream, Nancy gazed hungrily at Nick and boldly closed the gap between them.

It was no easy task to keep herself from kicking the other woman, but Toni managed. "Nick, darling, there's a man over there trying to get your attention," she said, clinging to his arm and urging him away from Nancy.

Music blared suddenly over the conversants, and Nancy moved quickly toward Nick. "Oh, that's Dan Brenner, darling, you remember him? He seems to want to talk to you about something to do with you shipping something for him. But you can do that later. Dance with me, Nicky. You will excuse us, won't you, Toni?" She smiled provocatively, challenging Toni with a raised eyebrow look.

Toni's hand itched to slap the smile from Nancy's face, and she wished she could forget where she was, and who she was, long enough to voice the thoughts running through her mind. She gritted her teeth, her hand clenching at her side.

Laughing softly, his hand closing over her fist, Nick leaned down to whisper, "Sheathe your claws, little tigress," and calmly swept her into his arms.

Toni drifted happily with him. She nestled very close while he guided her around the cloud they were dancing on, liking the feel of his brawny chest beneath her soft cheek. She knew they made a striking contrast, she in her pink gown that clung like a second skin and Nick in a dark suit that shimmered with green tones in the light; he large and powerful, and she of diminutive size. She felt safe and warm in his arms.

"We were going to find that back door. . . ."

Laughing like mischievous children, they ran hand-in-hand away from the ballroom, through a long, dark hall, and were almost at a door at the end of that hall when Catherine's voice arrested their flight.

"Where are you two sneaking off to?" she demanded.

"Uh . . . I was just looking for an empty bedroom, mother," Toni uttered the first thing that jumped into her mind. "Nick's been driving all day and he's bushed."

"Good thinking!" Nick approved in a hoarse, amused whisper, and Toni blushed, clearly understanding what he was implying.

"The bedrooms are all *up*stairs, Toni," Catherine said smiling thinly. "And I've already had your bags brought in from your car."

Without a further word, Nick pulled Toni behind him through the downstairs rooms and up the main staircase. After opening several bedroom doors, they spied their luggage.

Laughing softly, Nick scooped Toni into his arms and carried her into the room. Holding her cradled warmly against his chest, he bent down and kissed her, at the same time reaching back his foot to kick the door shut.

Toni woke with a start. Then she remembered, not only where she was, but also what had happened during the night. A warmth as disturbing as it was pleasant flowed through her, and she knew she was blushing. She turned to look at the man who had interrupted her sleep all through the night, and found his side of the bed empty.

"Oh, no!" Flinging off her covers, she started out of bed only to crawl under the covers again when she discovered she was minus one very necessary nightgown. Her eyes quickly scanning the room, she located her lovely pink crepe gown lying in a heap on the floor,

Nick's clothes not too far from it. She relaxed, and settled herself back on her pillow. Nick had not left her; he was probably in the bathroom. Taking a deep breath of relief, she closed her eyes and tried to sleep.

"Hey, sleepyhead, aren't you going to get up?" Nick was leaning indolently against the bathroom door. "If we hurry, we can grab a quick cup of coffee and then split before anyone else is awake. I know this bunch. They'll stay in bed until two or three in the afternoon.... And they won't have had half the fun that we did," he added meaningfully, laughing when he noted the blush that heated Toni's face.

She glanced up, grimacing at him. No one had the right to look so good in the morning. Nick was wearing tan slacks and a short-sleeved shirt of cream-colored silk that was open at the throat; a gold medallion was half-hidden in the mass of curly black hair on his chest.

Without stopping to consider how Nick would take such a comment, Toni complained, "Oh, how can you be so damned cheerful after not getting enough sleep?"

Nick chuckled. "Think back to why we got no sleep, honey, and then tell me why I can be so cheerful now."

Blushing, Toni left the bed on the run and ducked inside the bathroom.

She had to stop eating so much, Toni told herself firmly when moments later she discovered that the button on her green slacks—her favorites!—would not meet the buttonhole unless she held her breath. Throwing on a matching pullover blouson, she ran a quick comb through her hair and hurried down to join Nick in the kitchen.

"I was already starting to miss you," Nick said, holding out his arms the minute Toni stepped into the kitchen.

"What kept you?" he demanded gruffly, drawing her close to him.

"I had to comb my hair, silly."

"Whatever for? It looks better mussed," he teased, one big hand tousling her hair.

Laughing, Toni lifted her face and eagerly met his mouth. His arms tightened possessively around her, pulling her hard against him. His lips moved over hers in little kisses that explored her mouth, intoxicating her, making her head swim as they became deeper and more passionate.

"I want you, Toni," he breathed against her mouth. He kissed her again with a hunger that reignited the fire in her loins. Toni lifted herself on her toes, wantonly arching her body against his, thrilling to the feel of him against her thigh.

"You know now, don't you, darling?" he whispered between kisses. "Oh, Toni!" His mouth settled almost harshly over hers, parting her lips, his tongue searing hers as they met inside her mouth. Toni shivered with longing from head to toe. With a soft moan deep in her throat, she sent her arms around his waist and clung to him.

"What do I know, Nick?" she asked shakily when he lifted his head from hers. Last night and early this morning while they made love he had whispered endearments into her ear, had told her how much he wanted her, how much he needed her in his life, but never once had he said that he loved her. And she needed to be told that he did.

Nick's gaze softened considerably, but before he could answer her, Catherine entered the room and curtly informed him that he was wanted on the phone.

"Damn!" Simultaneously the word exploded from two sets of disappointed lips.

"They're waiting for you, Nicholas," Catherine added tersely, "and it's long distance."

Nick's tense features hardened ominously. "No one knew I'd be here," he gritted, glaring down at Catherine. Then he turned on his heel and stalked from the room.

"Goodness, Antoinette," Catherine growled disapprovingly. "Must you two always be pawing each other?"

The love haze in Toni's eyes faded abruptly. She supposed her mother was angry because they had not returned to the party last night. Her heart softened, and she began to apologize. "Mother, I know that what Nick and I did——"

Catherine cut in sharply. "It was rude and unforgivable of you, Antoinette. You left me in a very humiliating position, you know. There were people here who wanted to meet you, others who had been waiting to speak to Nicholas, and it was very embarrassing to have to tell them that you'd gone to bed almost as soon as you arrived."

"I'm awfully sorry," Toni agreed remorsefully, "but . . . well, you know how it is when you're in love and——" She stopped abruptly. Catherine's face had gone a sickly white, and her eyes were wide with an expression that terrified Toni.

"Mother?" Breast swelled with concern, Toni rushed across the room to take Catherine in her arms. "Mother, what's wrong?"

Catherine whimpered. "Oh, Toni, my baby, my baby." Her voice broke on a sob. "Oh, baby, this is dreadful." A great shudder overwhelmed her slender form, communicating itself to Toni. "Toni, if only I'd known ... I ... oh, darling, I'm so sorry!" Sobbing quietly, she pushed out of Toni's arms and stumbled across the room to collapse into a chair. She stuttered a plea for Toni's forgiveness.

Whatever for? Toni wondered fearfully. Her heart ached for understanding; she racked her brain for a reason to explain her mother's odd behavior, but it seemed her brain had gone into hiding. She could not think; she could not even find her voice to ask Catherine to explain what she was saying.

Erroneously taking Toni's silence for condemnation, Catherine went for broke in a stronger voice. She told Toni that everyone in her crowd had known Nick must marry before the year was out in order to stand even a small chance of becoming chairman of the board. When they learned of his marriage to Toni, everyone assumed that Nick had made some sort of business arrangement with her.

"I didn't want to think that you were that mercenary, Toni. After all, you have more than enough money as it is. But then again, I couldn't imagine why else you would want to marry Nicholas." Dramatically bowing her head into her hands, Catherine moaned. "Oh, darling, I never for one moment thought that you had fallen in love with him!

"And then ... last week ... when Nancy told me ... well, that he and she ... that is—" She shook her head; apparently she could not put words to what she was thinking.

Toni's mind slowly began to function. Catherine was implying that Nick had been cheating on her. "What makes you think he's been cheating on me, mother?" she asked, forcing calm to her voice.

"Oh, Nancy brags to me about everything," Catherine replied with irritation. "Why, I've known about her and Nicholas for simply ages now."

"I see." There were musical chairs, so why not musical beds? Toni smiled dazedly. She did not hurt, and it surprised her. She should be screaming in agony, or something. She had just had her worst fears confirmed and yet, here she stood, calm, not feeling a blessed thing. No pain, no regret...no, not even anger.

"Oh, darling, how I wish you had consulted me before you decided to marry Nicholas. I could have told you things about that man that would have made you not want to even speak to him!"

"Tell them to me, Catherine." Nick's challenge echoed harshly around the room. Catherine started, her eyes opened wide in horror as they swung to Nick's scowling face at the door. Numbly, Toni turned to stare at him.

His indolent stance was deceiving. He was like a predator, tense, shrewd, giving his prey the illusion of disinterest. Yet he was ready to strike, and Toni knew the recipient of his anger would be scorched deeper than if she had walked through a blaze.

"You!" hissed Catherine, finally finding her voice. "Why the devil couldn't you have found someone in your own league to put through this little charade of yours?" she demanded shrilly. "Why did it have to be Toni?"

"Because she was different from those women in what you so charmingly call my 'league.' Because she was very much unlike *you*, Catherine." His mouth was a taut line of anger. "Because from the very first time I saw her, she made it very plain that she didn't want anything *from* me. Because—" His gaze shifted to Toni, and his voice softened as he continued, "because from the very moment I saw her, with her hair mussed, a smudge of dirt on the tip of her nose, and her eyes blazing fire at me, I knew that I had to have her."

Pushing himself away from the door, he walked to where Toni was standing. "Let's go home, honey." Carefully, as though she would break if he went too fast, he took her in his arms, holding her lightly against him. Toni stood rigidly, unable to summon even a token struggle.

Nick's arms tightened fiercely, eliciting no noticeable response from Toni. He kissed her, bruising her lips with the edge of her own teeth as he pressed down in desperation, but her lips soured under his, and he knew it.

"You did a good job on her, Catherine," Nick muttered viciously, releasing Toni to turn to Catherine. He smiled, but it was not a pretty smile. "But you underestimated your daughter...again. Come on, honey, we're going home." He turned to find an empty space where Toni had been.

CHAPTER THIRTEEN

TONI STOOD ON the veranda of her bedroom and gazed across the bay of San Francisco in the distance, a kaleidoscope of silvers and turquoises and emeralds. As the night lights blinked on, a panorama of rich colors and patterns came alive before her eyes; the world below her hummed with activity and sparkled with city lights.

Nick was out there somewhere, probably having a whale of a good time. He should be here, she thought sadly, holding her, making her feel safe and secure. A wistful sigh escaped her lips without her realizing it.

She shook her head. Ever since the morning after Catherine's party, things between them had gone steadily downhill. After trying to clear the air more than once, Nick had given up and moved into his apartment in the city, presumably to be closer to his work. At least, that's what he said, and as long as Toni helped him maintain that pretense, no one seemed even to suspect that the Caldwell marriage was on the skids.

A small sigh escaped her when she felt the now-familiar queasiness in her stomach. She was pregnant. She ought to tell Nick, she owed him that, she thought as she stepped back into her room. But she could not. Each time she thought she had gathered enough courage to drop her little bombshell, something seemed to pull her back from the telephone. She would remind herself that Nick did not love her, so why would he care about the child?

He had not been to see her since he moved to the city, and when he made his obligatory weekly call, it was only to see if his checks were coming in on time.

His checks, she thought contemptuously, absently slipping on the dress she had laid out earlier that evening. She refused to cash them, stubbornly determined not to be obligated to him for anything.

Her eyes were darkened as they stared back at her from the mirror over her dresser. She did not want his money, she wanted *him!* As a substitute for him, *all* of his money was not nearly enough! she thought furiously.

"Damn him!" she muttered fiercely.

A wave of loneliness washed over her. She wanted him with her. She needed his arms around her, his mouth on hers. She ached with every fiber of her body to have him there, to hold her, to love away all her doubts and fears, to make her feel like a desirable woman.

Anger surged through her, stiffening her backbone.

"I'm going to give you one more chance, Nicholas Caldwell!" she told the silent phone as she stomped down the hall toward it. She lifted the receiver, dialing quickly before she could lose her nerve, and got Nick's answering service on the first ring. She gave the faceless voice a message for Nick, brief to the point of being almost rude.

Toni sensed a smile in the answering woman's voice as she repeated her message. "You want him to know you're on your way to New Orleans, and you don't know exactly when you'll be coming home."

"Exactly," Toni approved, smiling a trifle smugly.

It was a long shot, but it was all she had. It had to work.

If—and it looked like a mighty big *if*—Nick came after her, she would know that he loved her, and she would never ever nag him to put his love into words.

Toni's arrival in New Orleans went unnoticed. According to a note left on the front door for the milkman, Fannie had gone to visit friends for a few days, so Toni had the entire house to herself.

She took a bath, lingering in it until she felt and looked like a prune with her fingertips all wrinkled and white.

What if Nick did not come after her? nagged a worried little voice in Toni's mind, and her heart jerked at the thought. He had to come! He just had to!

Dressing in an old gown, part of the casual wardrobe she kept at Fannie's house, she decided to take a nap. Off and on she slept, but her dreams were all bad. She finally gave up, left the bed, dressed again, and went out for a walk.

She walked slowly, her hands clasped behind her back, her head bent forward, her mind fevered with worried thoughts. Had she made a mistake in leaving California? Should she have stayed, confronted Nick in his apartment?

No. She shook her head. She had done the right thing

in leaving. It was the only way she'd ever be sure that he loved her. Casting her worried thoughts aside, she walked to the edge of the river and sat down on the tall grass.

Night fell slowly over the huddled figure by the river's edge. Clouds pregnant with rain moved overhead, blocking the weak moon. Wearily, Toni lifted herself to her feet and went back to the house. After eating a spartan dinner, Toni went to bed. Perhaps tomorrow she would be able to think clearly, make plans, find an obstetrician, and start fixing up a nursery for her baby.

She turned fitfully all through the night, sleeping only for a few minutes at a time.

When Toni awoke, feeling tired and emotionally drained, the sun filtering through her window told her it was going to be a gorgeous day. Somehow that gave her a measure of contentment, and she left her bed with a smile. She bathed and dressed hurriedly in jeans and an old sweatshirt that hid the gap between the metal button and the buttonhole in her waistband. She went outside to sit on the porch swing while the coffee perked.

Nick found her there a couple of hours later, curled up with her knees drawn to her chest, her head cradled in her hands.

"Wake up, you scheming little witch."

Toni sat up with a startled gasp, rubbing the sleep from her eyes with her knuckles. She blinked. Nick was here!

The moment of disbelief mingled with sweet relief passed, leaving in its wake only a bittersweetness. Of course he had come after her! What a fool she was! In order for him to become *chairman* Nick, he would have to remain *husband* Nick.

Nick's eyes flickered over her. The expression in them was warm. "Am I so unwelcome a sight, Toni?" he inquired softly.

"What do you want, Nick?"

He smiled wickedly, suddenly looking relieved. "What I've always wanted since I first laid eyes on you, Toni—you . . . all of you."

He *would* say something like that, she thought angrily, refusing to believe him. She turned her face away and closed her eyes. She sensed Nick dropping down beside her, felt the swing dip with his weight, but would not turn to look at him. If she did, she would reach out for him, beg him to love her, and then she would never know if he had come after her only because he really needed her, and not because he needed her to help him win his miserable chairmanship.

Nick seemed to be in no hurry to speak. He leaned his head back and closed his eyes, sighing softly. Toni stole a look at him out of the corner of her eye. The dark tan of his skin made a startling contrast to his white silk shirt. His face was leaner and more uncompromising than she remembered. He looked tired, she thought, noting what seemed to be dark circles under his eyes. Very slowly he bent down and drew an envelope from the briefcase he had brought with him. Handing the envelope to her, he said, "To tell you the truth, Toni, I wouldn't have known what to do if I received any more little surprises like these." Giving her a smile that tugged at her heart, he leaned his head back again and closed his eyes.

Curiously Toni opened the envelope, and gasped when her hand brought out a stack of pictures. There were several shots of her and Dan Ramsey, in ambiguous poses, including the misleading shrimp-eating scene taken when they had lunched together. Then came insinuating photos of her and various male clients in a number of bars and restaurants around town. All very innocent, but if Nick chose not to believe her, all very damaging.

And why should he believe her, she thought with a sudden flash of insight. After all, he had tried to explain about Nancy, and she had not believed him. She swallowed nervously. He was obviously waiting for an explanation, and she did not know how to make him believe that she had done nothing wrong.

"I don't know what to say, Nick, except that I haven't done what these pictures imply." She held her breath, praying that he would say he believed her.

"I know, Toni," he said softly, and she expelled her indrawn breath in a sigh of relief.

The hands that wanted to reach out and shake the man out of his implacable calm she clasped tightly to her lap and waited for him to speak. And when he did not, she whispered, "How...where—" She shook her head. There was no need to ask where the pictures had come from. They had to have come from Nancy Kincaid.

"They were to be used to blackmail me into withdrawing from the fight for control of Caldwell," he said, the calm she heard in his voice surprising her.

Toni licked lips that were suddenly parched. "But how, Nick?" she asked in a voice that sounded alien to her ears.

"If," he started as he drew in a deep breath, "I withdrew—gracefully and silently—I would get the pictures and the negatives, and my stockholders would never know that not only had I not discarded my disreputable and reprehensible mode of living, but also I had married a woman who enjoyed—thrived on—that style of living."

"And if you didn't . . . ?" she interrupted, her throat tight with apprehension. Good Lord, he had not withdrawn!

"This—" he straightened, then bent to his briefcase and pulled out a folded newspaper. "It was printed especially for my benefit, to show me what could be done with those pictures."

Toni stared at the paper, at her smiling face as she looked up at Dan Ramsey. The caption was crude, suggestive; but what hurt her most was what it said about Nick's inability to keep his wife satisfied.

She felt defeated and deflated, and sick. Sagging against the back of the swing, she closed her eyes against the beginning of a throbbing headache. Lord, how could they fight something like this?

"Don't look so stricken, honey. They're not going to print that trash." Nick's hand went out, lightly caressed her cheek; with his thumb he gently dried a tear that had slipped out of the corner of her eye. "They did not count on Catherine's——"

"Catherine? Oh, Nick, surely you're not insinuating that my mother had anything to do with blackmailing you!" She sat upright and faced him, her expression daring him to say that Catherine *was* involved.

"No, darling. While your mother was far from innocent in all this, at least she knew nothing about the photos—not until the end," he said lovingly, his hands grasping her by the shoulders. Toni relaxed. "As soon as she found out about the blackmailing scheme, she somehow got hold of the pictures and brought them to me, together with the negatives and this," flicking the newsphoto of her and Dan with his middle finger. He shook his head, and Toni knew it was because he could not believe Catherine had done something to help them.

"I guess she loves you more than she hates me. And I'm glad. I can cope with whatever she dishes out, but not when she hurts you in the process."

Toni's heart was ready to explode with joy as she listened, but there was still something he was not saying.

"I was right about Nancy Kincaid, wasn't I?" she demanded, looking him straight in the eye.

"So was I, Toni, so quit looking so smug." He smiled grimly. "Regardless of what you might have thought, I knew all along that Nancy and Catherine were in league against me. But Nancy had some stock I needed, so I had to pretend ignorance." His expression was as serious as she had ever seen it.

"Their scheme was to get me married to one or the other of them. When that didn't work, they set out to destroy my position with the Caldwell stockholders through bad press. This Priscilla duPrie had never been a part of my life until one night when she suddenly appeared at my door in Paris. She was pretty, and I had been drinking. . . . Later I discovered she had been paid to do what she did—the whole of it."

Toni was confused. "But why did they want to ruin your chances at Caldwell?"

"You see," Nick explained, "there are two officers in the corporation who wanted to get rid of the shipping line because they know it's my pet. Each had promised to sell it to deAngeli if either one beat me to the chairmanship. DeAngeli has made several offers for the line, but I've turned him down every time. This——"

"I can see where my mother would benefit from Guido's gaining control of the shipping line, but not where——"

Nick's bitter laugh interrupted her. "Catherine and Nancy are in the same boat, honey. Nancy borrowed heavily from deAngeli to invest in fly-by-night businesses that went *kaput* shortly after she plunked his money down. And Catherine——" He chuckled dryly. "Catherine did not make out as well as you might've imagined by marrying deAngeli. He had her sign a marriage contract renouncing any and all claims to his fortune before he'd marry her. But as I understand it, he promised her a hefty bonus if he could get his hands on the shipping line. Nancy would have come out ahead too because her stock would have tripled if the deal went through. Of course, Catherine had no way of knowing that Nancy would stoop to blackmail."

Toni felt a tightness in her throat and turned away from him to hide the mistiness that had come into her eyes. She knew Nick was not lying about Catherine's involvement in the scheme to rob him of his precious shipping line. Catherine had always been greedy. What touched Toni now was that the entire messy business also proved—for the very first time—that her mother loved her. Catherine's need for money was so great— like a sickness, really—that only the most powerful feelings for Toni could have made her abandon the intrigue.

Toni didn't trust herself to speak. It was all well and good that Nick knew the photos were phony and she knew that there was never anything between him and Nancy, but where did that *really* leave them? Toni took a deep gulp of air. She'd been leery of letting Nick know her true feelings because she was jealous and vulnerable, thinking that Nancy was her rival. She saw now that her silence and anger had made things immeasurably worse. It was now or never. Tremulously, Toni turned to face Nick, ready at last to pour out her feelings, but he spoke first.

"I've been such a fool, Toni," he said miserably. "For so damned long I could not bring myself to trust you enough to let you know how important you are in my life. I've been alone...depended on just myself...trusted just myself all my life, Toni. It was hard for me to admit that without you, even grandfather's corporation means nothing to me."

Toni gasped in surprise. She ached to reach out and to touch him, to tell him that she'd always loved him, but something about his expression stopped her. She understood him well enough to realize that he needed to make his explanation—probably more for his own benefit than for hers. She placed her other hand on top of his, and waited.

"I thought I'd go mad with jealousy, Toni, and I used business as an excuse to postpone a reckoning. When I heard you'd gone back to New Orleans, I was so afraid I'd lost you. You see, I knew by then that the photos meant nothing....What a lot of time we've wasted, sweetheart." He leaned forward to graze her cheek with his lips.

"I know, darling," replied Toni. "I was afraid to show my feelings, just like you." Toni nuzzled even closer against Nick's shoulder.

"I know, too," Nick said mischievously. Toni drew away from him, puzzled. "You see," he explained, "I found out about your unofficial campaigning for me that night at Jana Cooper's house, and I realized that only deep feelings could have prompted you to do such a thing. Thanks to you, I am now chairman of the board of Caldwell Industries."

"I'm so glad you won, Nick." Smiling tentatively, she tried to summon the courage to tell him that she was carrying his baby, but he was in no mood for talking. Slowly, deliberately, Nick's mouth closed over hers in a tender, lingering kiss.

"Nick, there's something I have to tell you!" she spoke breathlessly as she wrenched her mouth from his and tried to move away.

"What is it, Toni?" He chuckled. "Some small wifely complaint that's been nagging you?" he teased, stealing a kiss from her parted lips.

Toni grinned. "You might call it that."

"What, love? Did I forget to tell you how very much I love you?" He grazed her lips with his, trailing them across her cheek and down to the sensitive spot behind her ear. "I love you, my meddlesome, scheming, troublesome, lovely wife." Then his mouth was crushing hers, his hands roaming possessively over her body, finding the hem of her sweatshirt, then going under it to caress her soft skin.

"But, Nick, darling, there's something I have to tell you," she said, pulling away from him, keeping him at bay with her hands pressed hard against his chest.

"Well, I like that!" he stated with mock fury. "I tell the woman that I adore her, and all she can say is: 'But, Nick, there's something I just have to tell you.'

"Good Lord, baby," he breathed against her lips, "the least you could do when a man tells you he loves you is to say that you feel the same way about him, particularly if he's scared to death that you don't!"

Grey green eyes opened wide in reaction and gazed into anxious green ones. Smiling, Toni said, emphatically, "But I do love you, Nick. I think I always have. But I do have something to tell you, only I don't quite know how to say it."

"Later, love, it'll come to you later." Cradling her in his arms, he left the swing and started into the house before he thought to ask where Fannie was.

"She's visiting friends for a few days."

"How sweet of her," Nick mocked. "Then it's just you and me." His mouth settled over hers in a kiss that was sweetly passionate and full of promise. Tightening his arms around his precious bundle, he walked unerringly into her bedroom.

"It's not just you and me anymore, Nick," she whispered softly when he placed her in the center of the bed. "In the not-too-distant future I'm going to give you a daughter," she told him as Nick lay down beside her.

She heard Nick's breath catch, and then he laughed, his breath was a cool caress against her mouth as he leaned his face over hers to whisper, "She couldn't be any more trouble than her mother has been." Laughing again, softly, he began to take off her clothes.

"Nick?"

"Ummm?"

"Why did it take you so long to come after me?" she asked in a teasing voice.

Nick frowned. "Because I had to wait and see what the stockholders decided." He smiled wryly. "You couldn't have chosen a worse time to leave me, Toni. When I finally got your message, I was on my way to the meeting..."

"And," she prompted when it appeared that he was not going to say anymore.

"I wanted to get on my plane and come after you right then, but I couldn't just chuck the whole thing. I hope you can understand that I had to wait and find out how they had voted."

Toni nodded. "But how did you find out what I was up to at Jana Cooper's?"

"Your friends at Three-oh-three Fircrest can't keep a secret," he teased. "And you were too obvious. They knew you were trying to make brownie points for me. Now, be quiet and let me get on with business!" he ordered with a grin, and settled his lips warmly over one very erect nipple.

"Mmmm, always business," she sighed, and smiled as she embraced him.

There's nothing more precious than your

Second Chance at Love ™

All of the above titles are $1.75 per copy

Second Chance at Love™

All of the above titles are $1.75 per copy

WATCH FOR
6 NEW TITLES EVERY MONTH!

TM

Second Chance at Love

TM